Babes in the Woods

Babes in the Woods

Maria Anne McIntyre

ISBN 978-0-244-85164-4

Find me online:
https://twitter.com/valentinosugas

Contact me:
mariaanne.sugamins@gmail.com

My dear reader,

I hope that you enjoy delving into the simplicity of this world that I have created, and that you find respite in it during times of hardship.

Through the thick branches overhead, Miel could see just a hint of the sky in the form of tiny slivers shining through the gaps in the foliage. This allowed an ample source of light to bleed down into the woods. No matter how bright that the sunlight was, it was always tinged vaguely green from the leaves, which cast a wonderful filter down onto the path that he liked to walk along.

At dawn, the scent of dew clinging to the ground mingled with the green lighting perfectly; and at dusk, the small patches of sunlight remained warmer than the shadowy stretches underneath the heavy vegetation. It was always enjoyable walking along the beaten path to admire the beauty all around him at all hours of the day.

Some days, Miel liked to visit the glen when it was dawn: rising with the sun, and warming his skin under the glowing rays as rich in brightness and as golden as his skin.

Dawn was when the birds appeared to sing sweet serenades to the sun, like hallowed praises slipping free from his lips towards Heaven itself. It was a time of worship for not only the little creatures, but also for him – as he flitted around the woods as quick as a swift and appreciated all of nature's blessings.

But some days, like right now, Miel liked to visit the glen when it was dusk; slipping into the woods, just like how the moon floated up into the sky, so the starlight reflected off the little stream that ran through it. As the sun set, the sky would turn as pink as his hair in parts, and he loved it when it did so.

Dusk was when the little creatures often went into hiding, curling up within their dens and nests to keep the darkness at bay. Perhaps, the darkness frightened them, but Miel was not scared of it. He quite liked the dull evening light and how it illuminated his path so softly, and he enjoyed darting through the shadows that the trees created like a firefly.

As it was, the sky currently visible through the gaps in

the foliage was a shade of bruised purple, and this signalled that night was fast approaching. The air was balmy, just the way that he liked it, and there was no scent of rain in the air to signal there would be a wet night or an incoming summer storm.

Miel could usually sense when the weather would take a turn for the worse because he could *sense* the ripples in the air, along with the changing scents that warned the little creatures to find shelter. It was never an ominous scent, rather it was a gust of fresh air that was at complete odds with the rumbling peals of thunder that followed it.

Tonight, Miel decided, was going to be a pleasant evening indeed.

Miel could feel hints of dew still clinging to the soil and grass, which had not been absorbed by the plants and trees – even now, at this late hour. Whenever he stepped down on a damp patch of grass, his toes would almost curl up from the sensation. He knew the wet soil would creep its way into the gentle creases in his soles. He *loved* the way it did that; the way that the soil would dry onto his skin so he had to roughly brush it free, the dry particles crunching and scratching against his fingertips.

Sometimes, Miel had to wash it free with the brook water, and that was even more enjoyable. The water was cool and it chilled his skin, but it cleansed him of all the dirt too.

Miel liked visiting the woods to tend to a shrine that was built deep inside it, hidden within the thick growths of pussy willows, camphor, and juniper trees in a small cave. It was an ancient thing – an open altar with a series of statues that was surrounded by the very wilderness – and he loved it dearly. He knew if he did not tend to the shrine that the mortals probably never would, for when he had first stumbled across it, it had been in a state of disrepair: unloved and abandoned to the ages.

Upon his regular visits to the shrine, Miel had taken it upon himself to tend to it as well as he could. He had no clue if the mortals knew that he was the one who had first cleaned the shrine and restored it back to its original beauty, on account of the fact that they were unable to see him.

Did they assume a caretaker in the village did so instead? Someone that crept into the woods to do their work in secret?

No, the caretaker of their unloved shrine was in fact a divine being, and they would never even know.

Some days, when Miel was tending to the shrine, children would play in the glen. They liked skipping rocks and dipping their toes in the streams, and they were always convinced that they were going to find fish in the babbling brook waters (that they never did.) Maybe they would scale the pussy willows as dares, trying their hardest to be the one to get to the highest branch, and worrying him so that they might fall and hurt themselves. Although he was busy with his own duties, Miel still enjoyed watching them out the corner of his eye. There was such a wonderful innocence in their actions and words – innocence that he knew mortals lost far too quickly.

Miel did not stop once on his dusky flit through the woods, his toes squelching in the damp soil and occasionally stepping down on a twig. They never snapped under his weight because he was so light and airy, nor did he even leave a print in the dirt. He only left a mark on the earthen plane when he *willed* it: like when he cleaned and tended to the shrine; or when he let his skin get coated in filth so he could clean it free. Otherwise, he passed through this plane like a spirit – a ghost haunting the woods.

A tree trunk got in his way, one that looked to have been felled by bad weather or even a large animal.

Miel could have ducked under it to get around the obstacle with ease. But he decided to go over it instead, giving his wings a hard beat so that he could soar up several feet to gently drop down on the other side. The only noise that he made was a low *fumph* from his wings, followed by a dull *thump* as his feet touched the ground once more. His soft, silken pink tunic floated around his thighs, as light as the feathers on his wings, before neatly falling back in place again.

A fox suddenly darted out of the bushes a few feet away from him, and she trotted right onto his path because she was on her own journey. There was a kit in her mouth, one that was clearly too young to trot on its own, and it was dangling limply in her strong hold.

Ah, were mother creatures not a sight to behold?

It was enough to make Miel stop so that he could hunker down and look at her. He eyed her magnificent ginger fur, and the flash of snow white on her muzzle, chest and tail tip.

"It is a beautiful evening today, is it not?" Miel asked with a smile.

The animal froze on the path for a moment, as if she had just sensed something out there in the glen. The vixen did not look at him exactly, she just stopped to scent the air with her wet, black nose. Miel saw her murky, golden eyes staring right through him as her ears turned erect, and even her brush-like tail fell still as she canvassed the area for threats. Then she resumed her trotting across the path, with two tiny kits hot on her trail hopping on their bumbling, black legs.

"Hmm, not as beautiful as you little creatures," he added, as he watched them go.

Miel thought that getting to observe the family of foxes tonight was a blessing, was something just for him – almost like a gift.

Perhaps he had earned the gift for his piety; not only in tending to this ancient mortal shrine, but for his daily duties? He sang sweet praises for hours and hours as he attended to whatever was required of him: be it listening to prayers, blessing the new souls that entered The Holy Kingdom, or the rare occasion of selecting which souls were to be reborn after their purification process had been completed. Sometimes, his duties were nothing more than tending to the pastures. But whatever the case, he fulfilled them with a smile on his face and a warmth in his soul.

This was why Miel liked to think that he was blessed to witness such treasures as these. Foxes, flowers in bloom, mortal children playing – these sights were all rewards for his endless devotion.

God is good, and God's gifts were constant reminders of this every single dawn.

It was as he was drawing close to the glen that Miel detected something unexpected, something that made his elation damper down.

There was a scent hanging in the air that made his body feel strange. It was not at all unpleasant to his nose, as it was obviously floral in nature.

But the scent was much stronger than what usually lingered in the air of the glen. His first thought upon catching the unusual scent was – gardenia, for it resembled that heady and sweet floral perfume that he knew well.

Usually, the glen contained the unmistakable scent of camphor from the trees, which was a scent that cleared the lungs and mind with its powerful purity.

Yet, Miel could smell gardenias layering over the camphor scent, and it was enough to make him slow his pace down.

There were no gardenias in these woods.

Miel had never seen them or scented them before, so where *was* the smell coming from?

There was something different this dusk, something unusual that Miel did not like. It made him feel strange, a little bit scared, in fact – even when he did not know why he felt such a way.

It was just a scent, and yet it carried with it the foreboding sense of dread. It was enough to make him reach up to clasp at his crucifix as he ducked his head under the low-hanging branches to enter the glen.

"... think mam will let you keep it," a child's voice declared; a boy's voice that was sweet and light enough to mean he was still small.

"Mam does not have to know," a girl replied in a somewhat spunky tone, signalling that she might just be an older sibling. She was certainly in charge, that much was obvious. *"It will be our secret, yes?"*

"Um, but she might get mad..."

"Ah, Edgar! She will not find out; we will keep it under the bed! Like we did with the frog, before it escaped."

"M'kay, sister," Edgar mumbled. *"You are right, 'cos you*

are so smart."

When Miel emerged through the trees, he saw there were two children in the glen, and they were currently hunkered down to look at something.

The girl, who looked older, had her sleek black hair pulled back and braided into a knot that was secured with several pins. She was wearing a pinafore of soft white over a blue dress.

The boy, who was much smaller than her, had a cap of black felt on his head. He was wearing deep-blue trousers with a white shirt.

Yes, just a glance told him that they were most certainly siblings, on the basis that they had the exact same button noses.

Judging from their excited but hushed whispers that he had heard a moment ago, they had caught a bug of some kind and were planning on keeping it in 'a jar' that their mother would never find.

A quick glance down at what they were studying revealed that the bug in question was a jewel bug, with a gleaming, metallic green and red shell covered in black spots. Like the creature's name suggested, it glinted like a precious jewel, and these children did not want to let it go. It was sitting on the palm of the little boy's hand, and it would soon be shifted into a jar for safekeeping instead.

Squatting down beside them, his knees drawn-up to rest his chin on them, and his hands loosely clasped around his ankles, was a stranger that Miel had never laid eyes on before.

Miel could see that the stranger was wearing a black tunic with short sleeves made of rough-spun cotton that looked to skirt around his knees. The tunic revealed his thin, lower legs and arms, which showed that he had lightly tanned skin.

The stranger's head was currently bowed to observe the children, and so Miel could not see his face at all – save for his bluish-tinged hair, and a hint of a rounded nose.

There, sprouting out of the top of his dark hair, Miel could see two little bumps that looked just like horns.

"Dæmon!" Miel exclaimed in horror, unable to control the

sudden urge.

At his cry, the dæmon looked up sharply so that they made direct eye-contact. His eyes grew incredibly round in what could only be fear, and then he shot upright to dart across the clearing and get away from him.

Miel instinctively ran into the glen, just to keep him at bay because he did not know what else to do. He had expected the dæmon would have ran away as fast as he could at the sight of him, and yet he had not. Rather, he had dived behind one of the pussy willows to cower behind its sturdy trunk.

Was this because Miel had not given chase when he was supposed to do so?

Was he supposed to banish dæmons in such a way?

Miel did not know what to do because he had never seen a dæmon before in his entire existence, and so he was just as frightened of the dæmon as he seemed to be of him.

Had it not been for those little horns, Miel might not have even *known* that the other being was a dæmon, for he had not looked very... monstrous to him. Not even remotely. But he was not going to think about such trivial things right now.

"Are you here to butcher these babes?" Miel asked, and he darted forward to shield the children behind his wings and outstretched arms – as if it meant a thing.

The children just resumed their act of bug hunting like there was nothing at all going on; they were completely oblivious to the fact there was both an angel and a dæmon in their midst. Miel even heard them laughing about something, just to show how ignorant they were to what was going on around them.

"I would never!" the dæmon exclaimed, and there was genuine shock and horror evident in his deep voice.

This exclamation caught Miel by surprise and made him slowly drop his arms back down to his sides. It made perfect sense to him that a dæmon would do such an act because it was vicious and cruel.

Yet, the dæmon sounded horrified that he would accuse him of such a thing.

Miel had not expected such a reaction from him, and for

7

a moment, he was rendered speechless as he tried to think of what to say in reply. "Then... then why are you here?" he asked, his fingers grabbing at the skirt of his tunic so he could play with the fine material.

Was it wise to ask a dæmon questions? Were they not supposed to be persuasive liars, and fabricators of tall tales that could fool mortals and angels alike? Whatever he replied with could be the truth, or it could be a grand lie, and he might not be able to figure out which one was reality.

Miel knew he should probably chase the dæmon away; but he was both curious and a little bit timid because of his sudden appearance in the glen. He did not want to banish the being without knowing why he was here, on this dusk just like every other – even if it was a bad idea. Just looking at the dæmon made his very being feel cold and weak, but he could not seem to fight the urge.

"I... well, I like watching them," the dæmon replied. He was still very much hiding behind the willow tree and refusing to look at him.

Did he think that he was going to hurt him, which was why he was hiding from him?

Miel did not think it possible that he *could* hurt something – even if that something was a dæmon and was therefore subject to heavenly wrath. He had never hurt a single soul, or any of the little creatures on this earthen plane, and so he really did not think that he could attack the other being.

Hopefully, the dæmon was too frightened to do such acts of violence towards him in turn, so that his potentially misguided mercy would not result in any grievous injury.

"You like watching them?" Miel asked in a soft voice, his fingers twitching around the silk. "Why? Why do you like watching them?"

For a moment, it seemed like the dæmon was not going to reply to this question. It was not like he had to; but it would most certainly help his cause if he gave him an answer that showed that he was not planning on hurting the children, and he did not want to cause any trouble. There was a chance that whatever he said could all be one elaborate lie, but this did not seem to matter to him at this moment.

Miel could sort the lies from the truth in time, should the other being linger long enough before fleeing off into the darkness once more.

"They cannot see me," the dæmon explained in a quiet voice. "If they cannot see me, they are not scared of me. That means I can watch them playing as much as I want, so I like to watch them. Sometimes, they say funny things, and they go on adventures and tell stories. It is pleasing listening to their stories, especially the ones with heroes and monsters in them. Often, they play games with strange and countless rules. I have seen plenty of first kisses too…"

The dæmon peered around the pussy willow to spare a quick glance at him at this.

Miel was granted another chance to look at him. He saw that blueish-coloured hair of his falling over a round face; and eyes that looked closer to black than anything else, with no hints of brown, blue, green, or other colours visible in their glossy surfaces.

"Why do you come here?"

"Why do I come here?" Miel repeated, before explaining. "Well, I come to tend to an ancient shrine just through the glen. But… I like watching the babes playing too. They *do* say funny things sometimes, and their games make no sense at all."

"Like the one with the colourful pebbles," the dæmon remarked, and his tone indicated that he might just be smiling.

"Ah, why do they throw them into the air like that?" Miel asked with a gentle head shake, his own lips lifting at the corners in a smile.

Behind him, the children made a sudden noise, and so he glanced back over his shoulder to look at them. They seemed to have succeeded in trapping the jewel bug in a little glass jar that had once held food or liquid, and this meant it was time for them to go back home again. Before their mother got worried or scolded them for playing in the dark (and possibly dangerous) woods.

The girl reached over to grab the little boy's hand, and she was obviously the oldest one because she was a whole head taller than him. Edgar obediently took hold and allowed her to guide him back across the clearing and through the trees.

This left them both alone in the glen.

When Miel turned back to the dæmon, he caught sight of him diving back behind the pussy willow once more. He must have been peering around the trunk to either watch the children or look at him. The fact that he was still hiding meant he was certainly scared of him, and Miel did not like this. He did not like the idea of anything being frightened of him, and not only because he was an angel.

Fear was a horrible emotion, and it made him feel cruel knowing that the dæmon feared him.

"I am sorry," Miel said to break the silence of the glen. "I was frightened, and I accused you of a horrible act without much thought. I should not have said that, about you butchering the mortal babes. But when I saw you, I just could not help myself."

"Did... did you just apologise to a dæmon?" he asked in shock.

"I... I did," he admitted with a nod. "It was wrong of me to accuse you of such things, no matter if I was frightened or not. You were frightened too, and I feel cruel right now. I-I am not going to hurt you, dæmon – I promise."

"Angels are strange beings," the dæmon mumbled in a whisper-soft voice. He was possibly talking aloud to himself. "Apologising, making promises; you confuse me greatly."

"Do you promise to not hurt me?" Miel asked, as he stubbed his bare toes in the hard soil. "I will take your word for it, if you promise me."

"I... I promise."

"May I ask the dæmon's name? You do have a name, yes?" he asked with a soft smile. He hoped that he sounded intrigued and not at all condescending towards the fellow.

"Do angels have names?" the dæmon asked him in return, and he peered around the tree trunk to look at him with those rounded, black eyes of his.

"We have many. I quite like one of them more than the

others – Miel. It is not my holiest name, nor one that my brothers and sisters often call me, but I like it. You can call me 'Miel,' if you desire?"

"Mi...el," he echoed, his eyelids rapidly fluttering. "Mmm, that sounds like a holy name to me, and you have got holier ones."

"I do. But they are not as easy or pleasing to say. Please, tell me that you have got a name too?"

"Dæmons are not given names – not true names," he explained, slowly moving from foot-to-foot behind the tree trunk. It revealed a little more of his face, but not all of it. "We are not loved enough for such things. But I gave myself one, a long time ago."

"You did? Well, that is good!" Miel declared with a happy smile. "I can call you that instead. What is it?"

"... Satariel."

"'Satariel?'" he repeated, the name flowing off his tongue so very smoothly. "Why ever did you pick that name, I wonder? I do not know what it means exactly, I have never heard it before. Do you know what it means?"

"No," the dæmon replied in a quiet voice, as he shrunk back behind the trunk again. "I do not know what it means either. I did not pick it for its meaning, I picked it because I... I liked it."

The glen fell silent once more, the pair of them standing in place and moving only to spare quick glances at each other.

Miel was on perfect display to the dæmon to allow him to study him. But Satariel was mostly hidden behind the pussy willow, and so he could not do the same to him in return.

What Miel had seen of him looked considerably 'normal' – save for the protruding horns – but he was curious enough to want to look at him more fully. This meant that he needed to draw him out, to instill in him more confidence so that he would stop hiding himself from view.

"I have never met a dæmon before, just you," Miel said, as he slowly crossed the glen to get to an old trunk that was lying across the middle. He had to beat his wings hard to float up and comfortably settle down onto it, his toes hovering high above the grass. "I do not know what is supposed to happen when we meet, not exactly. I suppose that most angels and dæmons would wage bloody battle at the sight of one another, as it is expected of us."

"Yet, you have not struck me down," Satariel remarked from his safety-zone behind the willow trunk. His cheek was pressed against the aged bark as he eyed him through the droopy branches.

"No, I have not," Miel agreed in a quiet voice.

"Why?"

Satariel's question lingered in the glen air like smoke, floating around them both as Miel slowly breathed it in. It was a perfectly reasonable question to ask, as it really was peculiar that they were talking to one another rather than spilling blood.

Yet, he did not truly have an answer to give him, or at least one that made sense.

"Well, I do not see why I should strike you down, or why you should strike me down either," Miel replied with the softest shrug of his shoulders, his wings gently twitching from the movement. "I have no desire to hurt you and, so far as I can tell, you have no desire to hurt me either. I like this mutuality; what say you?"

"I do too," Satariel admitted, as he finally moved around the trunk. He pressed his back up against the wood, but his body was fully revealed to him through the spaces between overhanging branches. "I am very grateful to still be breathing, I must say."

"Satariel?"

"Yes, Mi... Miel?"

It felt strange hearing his name coming out of the dæmon's lips like that; seeing his lips moving and not spilling out curses and hisses, or spitting venom at him.

Did Satariel find it strange when he said his name too, or was it just him?

Whatever the case, Miel was so very filled with curious questions that he knew he needed to ask. He had a feeling that Satariel might just be as intrigued as he was, and that he would be willing to answer them in return for his own questions.

12

"I was always told that dæmons look very different, not like angels or mortals at all."

Miel slowly ran his gaze down Satariel's black tunic to eye his normal arms and legs. They even had normal hands and feet on the ends too, along with perfectly formed fingers and toes.

"But you look... Well, you look just like me; I suppose?"

"What do you mean? What did you think I was supposed to look like?" Satariel asked, lifting his own hands up to look at his fingers as if he was curious too.

"I was told that dæmons look like monsters," Miel confided in a quiet voice. He hoped that he would not offend him with this statement. "You are supposed to have scaly skin, dark and tough like leather, and massive curved horns, claws and fangs. You are supposed to... to stink of brimstone, and your feet scorch the very earth. Most of all, you are supposed to be *very* scary."

For some reason, Satariel snorted at this description, and the sound carried clearly on the still air.

Did the dæmon find it amusing that he had naïvely believed such a thing; that his heavenly wisdom had been so very erroneous? What about his kind? Did they also have beliefs about what angels were supposed to look like, or not?

"Do I look like what you assumed angels to look like?" Miel curiously asked, lightly swinging his bare feet back and forth.

"I was told that angels can burn us to ash with a single look," Satariel said in a quiet voice. He was still avoiding his eyes, almost as if he was frightened this might just happen to him. "It is because you have flames in your skulls, instead of eyes."

Miel gasped, "That sounds frightening! Why would dæmons say that? You make us sound like... like monsters!"

"Because we are frightened of you; I suppose?" Satariel said, and he lifted his gaze at last to look up at him from across the glen. "Why do angels say that we look like that too – all scaly and hideous, with massive horns, fangs and claws?"

"Well, to make you sound like... monsters," Miel replied

13

in a quiet voice, the sudden realisation hitting him.

"I have never heard any other descriptions for angels," Satariel added. "Or at least none that I could believe. If you burn us to ash with a single look, how can any dæmon know what an angel truly looks like, mmm?"

Miel thought this over for a moment, and he suddenly became aware of how intelligent the dæmon was. He had heard they were liars and manipulators, but not that they were in any way intelligent beings like angels.

However, Satariel seemed very smart if he had reached such a conclusion – one that had yet to even cross his mind.

"But, in my mind, I have always imagined angels to be... big, blinding creatures that are bright enough to melt the skin off my very bones. Like the sun, maybe, should the sun have birthed its own children. Very scary, in other words," Satariel explained, and he reached down to tug at his tunic skirt in a fidgeting manner. "But you do not look like that at all."

"No, we both look just like each other." Miel lifted his own hands to look at his palms, and he saw that some dirt from the trunk was currently coating them. "It is strange, Satariel, it is very strange. Do you not think? If you did not have those horns, I do not believe that I would have even known you were a dæmon."

"If you did not have those big wings, I would not have thought you to be an angel either," Satariel admitted. "I mean, you glow a lot, but not enough to blind me."

"And you give off a strong scent, but gardenias are not exactly brimstone."

Miel paused for a moment, thinking about all the things that he wanted to say, but not knowing if he should outright speak such words. After some study of his palms, he lowered his hands with a soft sigh and decided to just be honest with the dæmon, as he really did want to have a conversation with him.

"Satariel, I have many questions, and I was wondering if I could ask them? Having never met a dæmon before, I cannot seem to help myself."

"Do you trust me enough to believe my answers? Even if

14

I might lie to you?"

"I do, I trust your word."

"Well, since you have not struck me down with flames, I guess that I should answer your questions," Satariel said, as he rubbed his hands all over the rough bark of the pussy willow. "It is only fair payment for my life, after all."

Miel wanted to tell him that he had not ever planned on smiting him down in flames. He had no clue how to do such an act, nor did he want to. But he had a feeling that the dæmon was already more than aware of this fact; and that his remarks were either little quips aimed to amuse them both or just simply because he was still in awe that he had been lucky enough to cross paths with him instead of a righteous angel that would set him alight.

"What do you care to know, Miel?"

"I am curious – do dæmons really eat hearts?" Miel asked, as he cocked his head to the side and studied him.

"Do little angels really sleep on clouds?" Satariel retorted without missing a beat, also cocking his head to the side to hold his gaze.

The question caught Miel by surprise because it was so quick, so witty. For a few seconds, he could only stare at the other being, but then he started laughing at the dæmon's wit. Never, in all his existence, had he heard such a thing, and it was so very amusing to picture in his mind.

Satariel looked shocked that he had made him laugh, as if such a reaction was unexpected, or even a little bit frightening. He shrank up against the tree that much more, almost like he wanted to morph through it and disappear from the glen, but Miel did not want that.

Not at all.

"We do not sleep on clouds, no," Miel explained with a slight smile. "I think that would be very comfortable though; what say you?"

Satariel made a soft noise at this, and his body relaxed in a way that showed that he was not scared of him, rather just cautious.

The dæmon had every right to be cautious. Miel would

try his hardest to ignore his unease, because he understood that Satariel had good reason to be frightened of him. He should probably still be frightened of him too, but upon seeing his fingers and toes, his tiny horns and smooth flesh, there seemed to be little reason to fear this particularly timid dæmon.

"Do dæmons eat mortal hearts?" Miel asked once more, pressing a little further because he felt like he could. "I hope to not offend you with this question, but I need to know if it is true or just another lie."

"I am not offended," Satariel replied. "An angel who apologises for accusing me of things is not the type to wilfully offend me now; is he?"

"I suppose not."

Miel could see the dæmon moving away from the pussy willow, and he was doing so ever so slowly because he was still uncertain. He took several creeping steps before reaching up to pull the branches aside, his hand gripping hold of the fuzzy grey catkins that coated the thin, overhanging branches. Then he finally slipped free from the bowers to stop hiding from him.

"Can I sit on the trunk too?" Satariel asked, clutching a catkin in his hand so that he could slowly stroke it. "I promise to not eat your heart, little angel."

The wry joke made Miel smile, and he moved to gently pat at the stretch of bark beside him to silently invite him to join him up on the trunk.

Satariel watched him doing so before he crossed the glen, stepping over the disturbed soil that the children had found their pretty bug in.

Satariel climbed up the tree trunk oh so nimbly, his fingers and toes slotting into the gaps in the ancient wood so that he scaled it like a little creature. A lizard, perhaps, though Miel would never call him such a creature for fear of angering him. As he reached the top, a strong waft of gardenia scent hit him that Miel breathed in deeply and held in his lungs.

"I have eaten mortal hearts, in the past," Satariel explained, as he settled in place on the trunk and delicately folded one leg over the other so he could place his hands on his bare knee. "When a mortal offers it to me in return for

16

earthly blessings, like riches of gold and paper, or the heart of another to be theirs, or to have talents beyond anything their kind has ever seen – I accept it as payment."

"What is it like? Eating a mortal heart? Does it have a taste?"

"Why, do you want to taste one too, little angel?" Satariel asked in return, cocking his head to look at him.

"No, never!" Miel exclaimed in horror, and he reached up to clasp at the front of his tunic.

Satariel held his gaze for a moment, his half-lidded eyes meeting his wide and glassy ones, and then the dæmon gave him a wicked grin that revealed bone-white teeth. It seemed his reaction might just have amused him, and Miel slowly loosened his hold on his silken tunic when he realised that the dæmon had been telling a joke. A quite disturbing joke at that, but a fitting one considering his nature.

It was at this exact moment that Miel also realised he was now able to fully look at his face, without a tree trunk or willow branches covering most of it from view.

Satariel had a very round face with a soft chin and high cheekbones. It was an unexpectedly youthful shape, all things considered. His nose was a gentle slope with a rounded tip, his lips were a small pout, and his eyes were framed by a thick spray of eyelashes that made them look delicate. However, his irises were jarring in contrast to his youthful and innocent features because they were as black as the night itself. They looked somewhat swollen, like they covered more of the whites of his eyes than they should have. But they were not as unsettling as Miel had expected dæmon eyes to look.

It was as he was studying his eyes that Miel noticed his own face was reflected in their dark depths. He was suddenly aware of the fact that Satariel could observe his face as intently as he had been studying his, and the realisation made him drop his gaze to look down at his rough-spun, black tunic instead.

"Mortal hearts taste like life itself," Satariel explained, closing his eyes and taking a deep breath to hold it in his lungs. "Some hearts taste bitter and raw on the tongue because the mortal has lived a bitter life full of envy, hate, and deceit. Some taste like honey, as sweet as can be, but a sickly sweetness that makes your mouth flood with saliva until it runs down your chin as drool. My favourite hearts taste spicy, pumped full of vigor and strength, because they make me feel powerful for a little while after consuming them."

"I see," Miel said in a quiet voice. "That is very... interesting, Satariel."

Satariel had just told him that his kind *did* eat mortal hearts; that this fact was not a lie or a mistaken belief that angels thought to be true. He had admitted it without a single hint of shame or disgust because he clearly did not believe he should feel such things. Why should he, being a dæmon and all? After all, eating mortal hearts was entirely normal to him – even if the mere thought horrified Miel.

How did he even *get* the hearts? Did he... tear them free from their chests with his fingers? Just thinking about it made him nibble on his lower lip, and Miel wondered if he should have asked Satariel such a morbid question to start their conversation.

"You asked me earlier about my name, about why I call myself 'Satariel,'" the dæmon said to break their momentary silence. "I could tell you, but I believe that you would not want to know."

"Why do you think that?" Miel asked, both curious and a little bit apprehensive of what he might just say in return. "You have told me about things I did not know about, like what hearts taste like. Why will you not tell me that?"

"Well, I am quite concerned it might frighten you," Satariel admitted in a quiet voice, as he stroked the furry catkin between his fingers and thumb. "Little angels seem easy to frighten to me."

"I do not think that you will frighten me," Miel replied, now even more curious because he really did want to know. Even if it might just actually frighten him. "Satariel?"

"I call myself 'Satariel' because it is the name of the first mortal whose heart I devoured."

Satariel held his eyes for a moment, blinking thrice rapidly, and then he dropped his gaze down to his lap. His

18

hands were loosely clasped together, and he started twiddling his thumbs in a manner that caught Miel by surprise.

There was something present on his features now, something that was not guilt or shame exactly, but maybe a poignant nostalgia.

It was strange that Miel felt something sympathetic towards the dæmon, even after knowing that he devoured mortal hearts, but he just did.

Perhaps it was the fact that Satariel could not *help* but devour hearts, as it was in his nature to do so. Dæmons were just like every other being in the end, subject to their own needs and cause for existence. Much like how the little creatures and mortals devoured one another; could he really be angry at a dæmon for doing the exact same thing?

Miel was a thinker, he always had been – a wise and loving angel, juxtaposed against his wise and wrathful superiors. Though he never asked questions in the kingdom, he never stopped thinking because he was cursed with an abundance of curiosity. His musings had brought him to the conclusion that hate was the most dreadful sin of all, for it was ungodly to hold anger in regard for anyone or anything. And so he could not find it in his heart to hate Satariel.

Maybe Satariel hated him, and he was just doing this to appease him and save his skin from harm?

Maybe not, Miel had no true way of knowing.

All Miel did know was that he was not scared of the dæmon, and he certainly did not hate him either.

"Did I frighten you with my answer?" Satariel asked, as he resumed his playful stroking and toying with the catkin. "I hope that I did not, I just wanted to be honest with you. Honesty from a dæmon must seem ironic, I know, but I was telling the truth."

"Honestly, you frightened me a little, Satariel. But you also made me more curious. How you described the ability to taste, for example, it fascinated me."

"What do you mean?"

"I cannot imagine such things," Miel confided in a whisper. "Flavours, tastes, the sensation of consuming something – it is unknown to me."

"Surely you eat, little angel?" Satariel asked, pausing in the act of stroking the catkin to look up at him.

"I, um, I do not eat," he explained, his gaze staring off across the clearing to study the pussy willow. "I do not need to eat. I have never felt hunger or the temptation to taste something before. So, I have never swallowed a single bite."

Satarial was quick to state, "Just because you have never felt hunger, it does not mean that you cannot eat. How have you existed for so long and *not* tasted something?"

"I do not know, I just have."

"An existence without taste or consuming things... I cannot imagine it." Satariel sounded as shocked as he had felt upon hearing about how he devoured hearts. "Can you feel anything? Can you enjoy sensations, or do you not experience these things either?"

"I can enjoy sensations. You come to this glen a lot, do you not? Often, when I am not present, I will bet that you come here too, to experience all of the sensations."

Satariel made a noise in response to this, a soft hum that revealed his assumption had been correct.

"Then you understand why I like enjoying the many sensations too," Miel continued, as he shifted on the trunk to fully look at him. "Like the sunlight through the foliage, casting down on you and lighting the way, or just simply warming your skin. Like the occasional dribble of rain, and the scent of it hanging in the air so sweetly, mingling with the flowers. And the flowers! Satariel, *the flowers!*"

For some reason, this made the dæmon's lips curl up at the corners into something close to a smile.

"When you can just smell them, hanging in the air when it is warm inside of the woods, so that every intake of air is just heavenly. It is a perfume made solely from nature herself, for mortals to enjoy. The little creatures that drink their pollen love their scents dearly," Miel said, and he reached up to cup his face in his hands and almost gushed in his excitement. "Sometimes, I feel like one of those little creatures because I love it so much!"

"What about the music?" Satariel asked, eyeing his little grin with a great fascination. "Have you heard the birdsong at dawn, when they come to life once more and all chirp and tweet different melodies, and yet–"

"They all layer into one beautiful song," Miel finished for him. "Or the cicadas at dusk, when they scuttle free and start their calling song, that strange chirping that's so very–"

"Haunting?" Satariel suggested, cocking his head so he could try and listen out for said call. "I like it a lot, especially when they–"

The dæmon suddenly stopped talking, his brow furrowed until the noise finally filled their ears.

Miel smiled at the distant echo of the cicada call; that high-pitched series of chirps that could have also been clicks growing in pitch like a crescendo before falling silent again. It sounded over the dissonant chirping of grasshoppers and other buzzing insects that he could not identify, bringing a static white noise to the glen so that it was not entirely silent.

Yes, haunting really was the best word for it because it was not like birdsong. It was not sweet, it was unusual and a little frightening to hear in the empty woods, but he still liked listening to it.

"You know what I love the most?" Miel asked with a wide grin, so caught up in his giddy burst of excitement that he could not help it. "Walking through the woods and *feeling* the soil on my skin, until my feet look like this–"

Miel shifted to lift his leg up and reveal his bare feet to him so that Satariel would be able to see the soil stuck on his soles. He had to plant his hands on the tree trunk and lean backwards to do so, his tunic bunching up around his stomach from the position and flashing quite a lot of his bare thighs.

Satariel eyed his soiled feet for a moment, his eyes rounded and running along the pads of his toes and the soft arch that led to his heel as he took in the sight. Then he reached over to grab at his ankle with one hand, catching him by surprise because he moved so fast.

Miel almost winced even when it did not hurt, because a part of him had almost expected that it would.

Having never met a dæmon prior to stumbling across Satariel, Miel had assumed that they were not supposed to touch each other like this; that it might burn his flesh to touch his kind, much like how his touch would sear Satariel's flesh too. He had always thought it would be forbidden for angels and dæmons to touch. Yet this seemed to not be the case, for his touch felt normal to him.

Satariel's fingers were cool and dry against his soles as he ran them over his skin, brushing at the still drying soil to knock it free.

Miel could not help but curl his toes up from the sensation, as it was somewhat ticklish. Looking at his foot, he was surprised to see how small that it looked in Satariel's hold, for the dæmon could easily cup his hand around the width of his foot and hold onto it. His toes looked so tiny, so fragile, next to his thumb, and he could probably crush his bones with ease – should he have wanted to do so.

But Satariel just brushed at the soil with his fingers as he ran his eyes over the sloped top of his foot. His foot was smooth and golden, with no hints of his fragile bones visible through his skin – save for his ankles – and the faint lines of his veins were traceable by both vision and touch.

Satariel lifted his hand to study his fingers and palms, eyeing the soil that was now clinging to his skin instead. He slowly rubbed his fingers and thumb together to feel the dry and gritty particles.

Miel's feet still had soil on them, which was trapped in the lines of his soles; but they were mostly clean now, thanks to him.

Satariel lifted his hand to his face, hovering it just below his mouth and nose almost as if he was... scenting the dirt. Miel would not be surprised if he was, for the smell was strong and intoxicating.

"Earth smells nice, do you not think so?" Satariel asked, closing his eyes and breathing in slowly. "I think I prefer it to the scent of flowers because it is so... raw, so ageless. I like breathing it in and thinking about how much decay the soil has absorbed; how many bodies have broken down to make it rich and fertile, just to grow more life. Nothing really dies, does it, little angel? Not in the true meaning, beyond the corporeal sense. The earth is immortal, and I love it as dearly as you love the flowers."

"I wish that flowers were immortal; but I suppose that their mortality makes them beautiful," Miel remarked, as he watched him dusting his hands free from dirt. "Some things are destined to die, and there is beauty in that."

"There is beauty in everything, if you look hard enough," the dæmon agreed, as he shifted to lean back on his own wrists and slowly lifted his feet to reveal them to him. "Sometimes, you must close your eyes to really *see* things without judgement, little angel."

Satariel's feet were also bare, and they were covered in dirt just like his. There was soil trapped in the light grooves on his skin, along with more obvious smears of green liquid from the grass that he had likely spent a lot of time walking in.

Miel usually walked along natural paths instead of through the grass, and so he did not often get grass stains on his feet. But Satariel's feet were covered in chlorophyll, and he was so incredibly tempted to reach down to touch his soles too because he wanted to feel that wetness on his skin.

Before Miel could help himself, he took hold of one of his ankles.

Much like how Satariel's touch had not burnt him, Miel was able to stroke his fingers and thumb over Satariel's foot without causing him any pain either. He gently ran his fingers over the pad beneath his toes first, before following the curve of his arch to feel the smooth and taut skin underneath the soil and smears of liquid. Unlike his hands, Satariel's feet were cold from the wet soil, and Miel liked how his warm fingers left a lingering residue of heat on the dæmon's skin.

Satariel's feet were larger than his, with more pronounced bones under his skin and longer toes too. The dæmon's hand had been large enough to cup his foot comfortably in his hold, and yet Miel knew that his hand was too small to do this. He could just about wrap his hand around his ankle, never mind cup the width of his foot in his hold.

As he ran his fingers along his sole, Miel reached up to caress his toes too, seeing them twitching from his touch. Then he lifted his hand to stroke the gentle slope of the top of his foot.

It was strange that a dæmon could have skin that felt just like his: smooth, soft and warm, rather than scaly, hard and cold. Strange, but nice.

Miel could not help but wonder what else was alike, seeing as their appearances and skin were one and the same.

When he relinquished his hold on his ankle, Miel's fingertips were now green from touching the grassy smears, but he did not mind at all. He liked it, for he could scent the clean and heady sweetness of the grass now on his skin. If he were to touch his tunic, the liquid would stain the silk, and so he tried his hardest to not do so.

"See? Sensations can feel nice, even when you do not eat," Miel said with a soft smile. "The one thing that I love more than feeling sensations is praising God with my voice. Ah, my body fills with warmth unlike any other whenever I sing praise, Satariel, and it makes my existence feel like a true blessing."

"I have never praised God before," Satariel admitted in a whisper, pulling his slight shoulders up almost in a flinch. "I have never praised anything, or felt blessed for existing like this."

Miel felt his smile slowly dying on his face at this. It was not hearing he had never praised God that had caused a sudden sinking sensation in his chest, but rather because Satariel seemed to be... bitter about the fact that he existed, rather than happy.

Could a being *feel* bad for existing? Miel had never thought of such a possibility before, but he had also never met a being as wretched and hated as a dæmon before either.

Should he ask the dæmon why he felt such things, or was that a question for another dusk – should they ever meet again?

"Well, I think that you should feel blessed you can observe the mortal babes playing," Miel suggested in a quiet voice. "Which you could never do if you did not exist, and you

24

could not enjoy birdsong and cicada calling songs either."

Satariel did not reply to this whilst he continued playing with the catkin, and Miel did not know if his words might have been upsetting to the dæmon. It was hard figuring out his emotions and possible thoughts from a glance because of those unusual eyes of his, and so he wanted to find a way of distracting him away from any potential upset.

"Satariel?"

"Mmm?"

"Can I touch your horns?"

At this, Satariel did so much more than look up, for he twisted sharply to stare at him with those funny eyes of his. They were rounded with surprise, and his lips were softly pouted in a little 'o' too. His stunned expression made Miel struggle to not laugh.

It was as if he had asked him something outrageous, and he supposed that it might just be outrageous for an angel to touch a dæmon's horns. But he had touched his feet and toes, so were his horns any different?

"Why do you want to touch my horns?"

"I have never touched dæmon horns before - I am curious!" Miel retorted, as he flashed him a rather mischievous grin. "Can I?"

"Can... can I touch your wings if you do? I have never touched angel wings before either," Satariel remarked, shifting his gaze over to look at his wings.

"Of course, touch them now if you want. I do not mind."

"Uh, you touch my horns first," he suggested in a low mumble, dropping his head for him.

Miel lifted one of his hands out of his lap and reached over and hover his fingers above his head of tangled and tousled dark hair.

Just about visible from the top, sprouting out on softly curved angles, there were two little protruding horns. They were thicker at the base, curving up to a tiny sharp point, and they had slight notches in them, rather than a smooth outer layer.

When he touched one of the horns, Miel found it to be warm and slightly rough against his skin.

"Oh..." he breathed out softly, as he rubbed along the hard bone-like surface so he could feel every bump and notch against the pad of his thumb.

Satariel made a little noise at this, but his head was still bowed and so he could not see his face. The dæmon might have felt his touch, he supposed, and maybe it was ticklish or unpleasant?

"I like how warm that they are," Miel said, and he clasped the other horn in his free hand to hold onto both horns. "I thought they might be freezing cold, or maybe scorching hot. But they are just warm instead. Can you feel that, when I touch them?"

"I can feel it, yes," Satariel replied, his own fingers lightly curling up and then loosening with twitches in his lap at the end of every rub of his thumb.

"Does it hurt? Should I stop?"

"It does not hurt, it is alright. It is kind of ticklish, I suppose? No one has ever touched them before, but I do not mind. Just do not tug on them, or tap them."

"Tug on them? That would be cruel," Miel said, as he slowly moved his thumb closer to the pointed tip.

"Do not touch the tips either or you will cut yourself! They are really sharp, I have cut my fingers on them before, by accident."

Rather than test his luck and pierce his poor thumb, Miel decided to let go of his horns and finish his impromptu investigation. Just like touching his skin, he had been able to touch his horns without feeling a hint of pain. Even they had not been cold and scaly, like he had always imagined dæmon horns to be.

"Here," Miel said, as he shifted on the trunk and turned on an angle to reveal his back to him. "I will warn you, my wings might move if you touch them. But do not be scared, they cannot hurt you. They just do that, sometimes."

"Do you not have control over them?" Satariel asked, and as he shifted on the trunk was an audible rustling sound from his tunic.

"I can control them whenever I want. But sometimes,

they like to twitch or ruffle, just like how our fingers or toes wriggle on their own," he explained, as he waited for him to finally touch his wings. "It must sound strange, but it is true, and–"

When Satariel touched his wing at last, he chose the right one, and he reached out to place his palm down on the feathers without much thought at all. The weight and heat of his palm was enough to make his wing twitch in response, ruffling his feathers with a hard *huff* that made the dæmon gasp loudly.

"It is alright," Miel continued with a soft laugh. "Just go slow, or use the back of your hand to not tug or ruffle them too much."

"Like... like this?"

Miel felt Satariel's touch on his wing once more, but this time it was cooler than before. He was using the side of his hand to stroke at his feathers instead of his palm, and he did so tantalisingly slow.

"Like that," he agreed, as he closed his eyes to better track his touch. "Like your horns, I guess that my wings are a little ticklish too. They have been touched before, when I preen them, but... I am not sure if my brothers and sisters have ever touched them. I cannot seem to remember."

"They feel different to what I expected," Satariel said in a quiet voice. His touch slowly moved down to his sharply tapered flight feathers, before he lifted his hand to start stroking them again from the very top of his wing. "They are warm, they are kind of soft, but also tough in parts."

"That is because each one has a different use. The tough ones? They are probably my contour or flight feathers. They keep my wings clean, and they help me fly. Underneath those ones, you will find–"

Miel paused as he felt Satariel lifting some the contour feathers on his ulna so he could try and locate what he was talking about.

"That is my down feathers; they keep me warm," he finished.

"Oh, they feel like... like dandelions," Satariel said, before laughing softly. "I did not know that angel wings were so intricate, so delicate."

"Delicate? I always thought they were tough," Miel said, as he slowly pulled his legs up in front of him to rest his feet on the trunk. The new position allowed him to hug his knees against his chest. "Why do you think that they are delicate?"

"Because the feathers are so soft and thin, and they are just like bird wings, only bigger. I always thought that angels had wings made from bone and leather, because then they would be strong and powerful. But your wings are so delicate and warm, little angel."

"Satariel, why do you keep calling me that?" Miel asked in a quiet voice, his cheek comfortably resting on his knees.

"Mmm?"

"Why do you call me 'little angel?'"

"Well, you are an angel and you are little," Satariel replied in a matter of fact voice, his fingers stroking along his left wing.

This made Miel laugh softly, despite not knowing why.

When Satariel had first used the term, he had assumed it to be a joke, a taunt perhaps – even when he did not seem the kind to do such things. But then he had kept using it, and it had seemed to have just stuck to him as a nickname.

"I do not think that I am that little, and you look little to me too, Satariel," he replied, opening his eyes to glance across the clearing again. "You are not exactly a *tall* dæmon, are you?"

"Pft, I do not have to be tall, I scare mortals to death just the way I am," Satariel retorted with an audible smirk in his tone. "Are angels supposed to be tall?"

"Um, maybe? I do not know– I am not little!" Miel argued, twisting to look back at him from over his shoulder. He had to twitch his wing to be able to peer at him, and the sudden movement caught the dæmon by surprise. "Even if I *am* little, at least I am quick and light on my feet, and I can fly fast."

"See? Little angels are just as good as big angels," Satariel said, as he lifted his hand to touch his wing again. "Just like how little dæmons are just as good as big dæmons."

"I do not think that there are any... endearments for dæmons," Miel replied, softly furrowing his brow. "The word

28

itself is negative, and I feel that any endearments using it are therefore cruel."

Satariel was quick to remark, "I do not find the word to be bad. I am a dæmon, I do not think it is bad for you to call me that, even if other angels hate me for being one. You do not, so, I do not mind you calling me that. But why are you giving me an endearment, mmm?"

"Because you gave me one. Little angel is an endearment, is it not?" Miel asked in a soft voice. He hoped that he had not wrongly assumed it to be a nickname, when it was in fact something else.

"I suppose it is," he agreed, as his fingers slipped underneath his contour feathers to locate his down feathers and stroke at them once more. "How funny we both are – giving each other endearments, and talking with and touching each other instead of fighting to the bloody death. Miel, I think that we are both a little hopeless."

"Hopeless, maybe. Or maybe, we are just too kind for such actions?"

Miel was so distracted by his stroking fingers that it took him a moment to realise that Satariel had grabbed hold of one of his flight feathers, and that was when he felt a sharp twinge of pain shooting up his wing. It was enough to make him gasp and jerk on the tree trunk, twisting around to stare at the dæmon in surprise.

Satariel eyed the pink-tinged feather that was stuck between his finger and thumb – the one that he had just plucked free without warning. It was long and sharply tapered into a slanted point, with a sheen on the smooth surface and countless little lines crossing across the body that connected to the barb.

"Do you think I am kind?" Satariel asked in a whisper, lifting his gaze from the feather to hold his eyes.

Miel held his gaze unblinkingly, once more seeing something in the dark depths of his eyes that was hard to read.

Was it mischief perhaps, a naughty streak of ill behaviour that all dæmons possessed?

Was it really something that he should be frightened of –

a potential for danger or cruelty?

Miel did not know, but he liked to think that whatever was glinting in the coal-black depths of his eyes was in fact something kind and gentle; something redeemable, or even hopeful.

"I think that you are kind, my dearest dæmon," Miel replied after a moment of thought.

This made something flicker across Satariel's face, and his brow furrowed for a second before his lips quivered. His fingers instinctively reached for the feather in his hand so that he could touch it, could stroke at it as he glanced off across the glen.

Satariel seemed to be surprised by the term 'dearest dæmon' – as if he had not expected him to say such a thing to him. Yet after a moment, his lips lifted at the corners into a smile that showed he had liked it.

"Do you come to this glen often, little angel?" he asked, as he resumed playing with the feather and gently stroked it alongside his chin and jawline.

"Every single day, if I can," Miel replied. "Sometimes at dawn, sometimes at dusk. I tend to the shrine here; it is part of my daily duties. What about you?"

"I come here every now and again, but I think that I am going to visit it more often now that I know it is a haven," Satariel said, the feather creeping up to brush against his cheek. "Supposing that the shrine caretaker does not mind, of course."

"I do not mind, not at all."

"Night is fast approaching. I think that it is time I left you to your duties; mmm, little angel?"

"Well, you can leave it you want, or you can stay. I do not mind," Miel said, as he hopped down from the tree trunk and felt his feet bouncing in the springy grass with a soft thumping sound. "Do dear dæmons often hide at nighttime? I thought you would like it the most?"

"Nighttime is a lonely time, a time for reflection and silence," Satariel replied, as he slipped his feather down inside his tunic to free up his hands. "It feels unusual talking to

30

another soul; do you not think so?"

The dæmon moved to scale down the tree trunk again in that quick and efficient manner of his, his toes and fingers not failing him once in locating nooks to use to get back down to the earth beside him. As soon as he was back on his feet, he tugged at the skirt of his tunic and wiped his dirty palms on it without a single care.

"If you come here tomorrow at dusk, you might just find your nighttime less lonely again," Miel said with a soft smile. "I think I would like to talk to you some more, Satariel. I have so many questions, after all, and I think you do too."

"Oh, little angel, I am sure that I could teach you about so many things," Satariel remarked with his own smile. "Maybe, about things that angels are not supposed to know about."

Miel watched the dæmon disappearing into the shadows around the glen, almost melting into the darkness like liquid night so that he lost sight of him in a mere blink.

As he lingered beside the tree trunk, it crossed Miel's mind how peculiar that their encounter had been.

Why, he was still struggling to believe the fact that he had met a dæmon on this very dusk. In all his existence, he had never imagined meeting one, and his knowledge of them had made him terrified of the very thought.

But Satariel had been nothing like his ignorant assumptions, and he wondered if the dæmon was also shocked by how different that angels really were now that he had met one too.

"A little dæmon indeed," he said to himself, before laughing under his breath.

Miel listened to the sound of the cicadas for a minute as he absorbed the evening atmosphere of the woods. If not for the little creatures' constant chirping, he imagined the silence would be heavy and unpleasant, and so he was thankful for their song blessing his ears.

The scent of gardenia was still hanging in the air – a ghostly perfume that the dæmon had left behind in his wake that might disappear on a soft breeze, or might linger for the remainder of his time in the woods.

Miel decided that it was time he finally tended to the shrine, which was set just through the glen in a little cave. He was in the act of skipping his feet over a scuttling beetle when he noticed something.

There, clinging to the skirt of his tunic, Miel could see a smear of chlorophyll from his hands. He must have accidentally touched it at some point during their conversation, and he just knew that the pink silk would never be free of the stain.

II.

Unlike the previous dusk, which had been a balmy night that had filled the woods with the warm scent of flowers, the scent in the air was completely different, and so it created a new atmosphere in the glen. This evening, there was a rich petrichor scent that Satariel greatly enjoyed; he enjoyed it more than the perfume from the flowers, in fact.

Breathing in the mineral rich scent let him know that it had rained on the mortal plane during his slumber. From what he could detect, it had been a heavy fall of rain. Not only in the strength of the scent, but because he could see raindrops still present on the blades of grass and leaves of the forest too – little translucent beads sitting on the waxy surfaces because they were too stubborn to run down and soak into the soil like the rest.

When Satariel took a deep breath and held it in his lungs, savouring the aromatic fragrance all around of him, he could not help but also recall another… potent scent.

It was still clinging to his skin, just like the raindrops were stuck to the grass and leaves. It was not a scent without taste, and it was still something that he was unable to rid himself of.

The taste of mortal blood was on his tongue: thick, oily, and very metallic. It had coated the surface of his mouth, and it was still trapped between his little sharp teeth and around his gum line.

Satariel slowly ran his tongue around his mouth to chase after a dribble of blood. It was enough to make his mouth flood with another burst of saliva, which mingled with the blood until it was a thin trickle that he greedily gulped down.

For quite some time now, Satariel had been trying his damnedest to rid himself of the blood, but it just would not go away. Even after scrubbing his hands in the brook water to get it out from underneath his nails, he could still see faint red lines trapped under them that he could not scrape free – not even with his teeth and sucking mouth. He could gulp down as many mouthfuls of bloody saliva as he needed until his mouth was free from gore, but sadly, he had yet to find a way to rid himself of those little traces of blood.

Satariel did not like how the scent of blood would stick to his skin for days afterwards: a constant, coppery scent that bade he dirty his hands with more of the hot substance. He especially did not like the fact that he stunk of blood when a certain angelic being was present in the woods once more.

An angelic being that could smell gardenias coming from his body in strong wafts and would no doubt detect the sinister scent on his flesh too. He seemed to have a fantastic sense of smell for a being that had never tasted a single thing before.

From his position in the shadows, Satariel could hear Miel inside the cave, but he could not see him. To catch sight of him, he would need to enter the cave, but he did not think he could do that on account of the hallowed shrine that was hidden inside it.

Satariel could sense pure and holy waves coming from the small mouth of the rocky shelter, and this was enough to frighten him away from possibly trying to enter.

Dæmons and holy ground were not exactly a match made in Heaven...

Had Satariel have stayed a little longer with the angel last night, he might just have felt emboldened enough to try entering the cave and looking at the shrine. Miel had filled him with a strange sense of bravado that he had never truly felt before, ever since he had discovered that he could touch angels and not be consumed by wrathful, holy flames.

After all, what danger was a holy shrine if he was able to touch the holy being that cared for it?

Though Satariel had left Miel to tend to his duties, he had not left the woods last night... not at all.

No, after darting through the trees and sinking into the shadowy shelter their trunks and branches had offered, Satariel had remained hidden from sight to resume observing Miel.

He had been unable to help himself because he had been so very curious and somewhat scared of what had happened between them. He had *needed* to observe him that little bit more, just to reassure himself that the angel was real *and* as kindhearted as he had seemed.

Satariel had not been lying to Miel when he had told him about what he had heard about angels. It might have shocked Miel to hear about how terrifying dæmons had claimed his kind to look, but the angel's description of his kind resembling massive, scaly, and horned monsters was just as shocking to him. He had never seen such a being in all his existence, and Satariel himself would have found a leathery-skinned monster with massive fangs and claws incredibly frightening.

Yes, though Satariel had not truly believed the stories about angels that he had heard, he had had no other knowledge to draw upon when he had been discovered by Miel. Therefore, a part of him had almost expected the other being to have had twin flames burning away inside his skeletal skull, along with massive, leathery wings the height and width of the camphor trees. He had thought that a single look would have caused his flesh to boil into liquid, before igniting until he died an agonising death – screaming the entire time.

Satariel had been terrified when he had realised that he had been caught by an angel, and he had honestly thought that he was going to be consumed by flames. But Miel had not looked anything like those old stories had claimed, not at all, and his appearance was not the only shocking thing.

Last night, Satariel had learnt that angels could touch his kind without setting them alight like living candle wicks. Maybe it was Miel's choice to not hurt him that meant he had been able to touch him, or maybe the holy beings could not actually do that with their touch. He did not know, but he did know that he had such warm and soft hands, and he had liked it when he had run his fingertips across his skin.

Angels and dæmons could touch one another.

There was nothing in the ancient scriptures that Satariel had ever read that had explicitly told him their kinds were forbidden to mingle or touch. He had no clue what knowledge that Miel might have on the matter, but the angelic being had seemed as clueless as he had been upon meeting him last night. It seem like they had no need to worry, but Satariel could only hope that he not suffer in any way because of him.

The last thing that he wanted was for Miel to be punished by his angelic brethren for his kindness, as that was too cruel to even imagine.

Miel needed to leave the shrine cave so he could finally see him again, but he must have a great many tasks to do before he was finished tending to said shrine. What those tasks might just be, Satariel was clueless, but he just needed to be as patient as he could and let the angel complete his daily duties. At least he could still *hear* him, and that was something he had been savouring since he had started hiding in the shadows.

Miel *sang* when he attended to the shrine, and he sang in a sweet voice that made Satariel's very being feel things that he had never felt before. The angel had spoken of being blessed to be able to pray and feel sensations, and getting to hear him singing made him feel like... like he might just be blessed too.

It was a strange sense of being *lifted* in some way, like his spirit was being revitalized and any lingering aches in his bones were being soothed away by that mellifluous and heavenly voice of his.

So soft, so sweet and flexible – how it would shift in pitch to the airiest of sighs that made his fingers weakly tremble at his sides.

Oh, there were really no words that Satariel could pluck out of his mind to describe how beautiful that Miel's singing was. Even when he was singing praise, which was something that should have disgusted him, or even caused him trauma in some way, Satariel felt so content listening to it.

Being outside the cave, he was not even hearing the full quality of his praises, but rather an echoed and faintly distorted version. But even that alone was perfect to his ears.

Miel was singing melodies without words or meaning, and making beautiful sounds with his tongue and throat that transcended the need for words. It was something that even Satariel himself would be capable of doing, but he would never attempt it. His timbre was too deep and... rusty to produce such honeyed sounds, and he would feel great shame if Miel were to hear his bumbling attempts.

Satariel closed his eyes just as Miel's voice swelled into a powerful note, which soared through the air and made him wish that all the little creatures in the underbrush could be touched by the harmony. It was enough to bring chills down his spine, and his fingers clenched so tight that his nails dug into the skin of his palms.

As the note slowly descended into stillness, Satariel opened his eyes to see that Miel was emerging from the cave. He wanted to burst free from the copse of trees and greet him. Yet he found his body growing heavy and stiff at the mere sight of him. He even shrank back against the trunk of the pussy willow, longing to melt through the rough bark and hide his body from view through the drooping branches.

Miel was glowing, so radiant and angelic, and he was a shade of being – a lowly and cold dæmon, with the taste of blood on his tongue and ugly little horns. He should not disturb the angel like this, and he should not trail along behind him like a puppy demanding attention and affection because he would only sully that radiance of his; he just knew it. That wonderful heat Miel exuded would be sucked up by his greediness, just to warm his weary, old bones again.

But Miel had been so curious last night, so curious and eager. Had Satariel not seen wonder in those powder blue eyes of his; as he had gazed upon his face without judgement, without hate? Had the angel not touched his cool flesh so tenderly, tickling at his toes and stroking his horns with such care and fascination?

Maybe Miel's warmth and radiance might not be stolen by him, but rather... shared?

Satariel took a deep breath and held it in his lungs, finally plucking up the courage to step out from behind of the pussy willow to let Miel catch sight of him through the branches.

It took the angelic being a moment to do so because he was so distracted gently cleaning his hands free from dirt, but when he happened to look up and see him, it was enough to make him freeze in place.

"Oh, you came back?" Miel asked, his shoulders and

wings lifting up in something that looked like surprise. But then a smile appeared on his lips and they relaxed again, his feathers ruffling softly before falling still.

"I... I did," Satariel replied, stubbing his bare toes in the damp soil. "Were you tending to the shrine? I have never went near it, of course, but I know that it is inside that cave."

"I was," he agreed with a nod. "My duties are to clean it free from dirt. Leaves and debris blow inside the mouth of the cave over time, so I clean it all away to ensure that the shrine remains pure. Then I cleanse the altar with water, and I pray because I like to. The praying is not part of my duties, just my way of giving thanks."

Satariel made a noise at this, a soft hum to show that he was listening to his words intently.

He wanted to say something more, to continue their conversation, but there was little that he could say in regards to things like cleansing altars and praying. He did neither of these things, he never had in his entire existence, and so it might be wise that he remain silent on the subject so that he did not offend Miel with his ignorance.

After a moment of studying his bare feet, Satariel decided to glance up and look at the holy being.

Miel was not blinding, like he had feared he would have been. But his skin *did* glow in a way that was supernatural. It was subtle: a rosiness to his full cheeks that was just a little too bright; a warm undertone to his golden skin so that it seemed to radiate light and heat into the air like a halo.

The angel's eyes were a soft blue shade, droopy and heavily-lidded in a Byzantine fashion, but they seemed to be sweet to him. When his eyelids crinkled deeply at the corners, they certainly looked more youthful. His nose was slight with a sharp point to the tip, just like his jawline, but his plush lips and full cheeks softened his pointed features somewhat. His gainly limbs, bare from the sleeves and skirt of his tunic, also added a youthful charm to his appearance.

Miel's hair was a pink as vivid as the dawn skies when sunlight started to bleed into the clouds; but his lips were a much duskier shade – dark, rather than light. Just like his silken tunic of pink, which reflected the dull light that shone through the foliage and never seemed to be one shade but a myriad of hues, his wings were not simply white.

No, whilst Satariel had been playing with his feathers at dusk, he had discovered that Miel's wings were tinctured with dozens of resplendent colours. They might just look white on the surface, but upon closer inspection, and right when the light touched the surface of his feathers, they revealed to him a rainbow that he had never expected.

Miel's flight feathers, with their razor-cut tips and strong coating, were tinged with shades of pink from the edges up to the very root that connected to the barb. Some of them had been as vivid as his hair, some had been dusky like his lips, and others had been a beautiful, gradient scale that he had found stunning.

Satariel had plucked one of the gradient feathers free just for himself, and it was currently dangling around his neck on a leather thong like a hallowed talisman: an angel feather charm.

His contour feathers, now they had been a sight to observe. They had covered most of his wings, from the base scapula joint to the very tips of his metacarpals, and along his thick humerus and the thinner delicate radius and ulna. They had made his wings appear golden in parts. Some of the rounded feathers had been gold tinged with threads of yellow, whereas others had been mixed with copper, and every single one of them had been beautiful.

Satariel could have plucked one of them instead, but the pink flight feathers had reminded him of Miel's hair, and so he had decided to not pluck one of the golden contour feathers.

The final hidden treasure had been Miel's down feathers, and those bundles of cotton-soft fluff had been as white as snow. Silver and blues had bled into the bundles just like clouds, or ice when it settled on lakes in a thin film.

Satariel had not wanted to pluck any of them, because they had been so soft that he had been frightened they would have crumpled in his hold and blew away in a soft breeze like dandelion spores. But they had been so very pleasing to touch, warm and fragrant with a scent that he thought might just be hibiscus: soft and sweet, but not powerful.

Satariel had quite simply enjoyed stroking all over Miel's wings to feel the different sensations with his fingertips, whilst also seeing shades that he had never seen before in his entire existence. He had no clue at all if Miel had found his horns as fascinating as he had found his wings, but he was certain that the angel found other aspects about him much more interesting.

Like his knowledge about tastes and the sensations that he liked, or the fact that he was learning all about dæmons from him.

"Did you just arrive, my dearest dæmon?" Miel asked, as he finished brushing his hands free of dirt and glanced up at him.

"I did, little angel," Satariel replied, still finding the endearment unusual but pleasing.

"Hmm, you must smell very strongly then, because I have been breathing in that gardenia scent of yours the entire time that I have been tending to the shrine," Miel remarked with a knowing smile, reaching up to rake his fingers through his hair. "How... peculiar."

Rose petal tellin, that was what came to mind when Satariel looked at his hair – that exact shade of pink, just like the seashells that fringed shorelines and were washed clean and glistening by the lapping tides. The dusky moonlight just made it shimmer that much more, and turned it into a beautiful shade he wondered if he could find on flower petals.

Satariel was aware that Miel knew he was lying to him, and that he might just have known he had been hiding in the shadows to watch him. But he felt no need to bluster out more lies and excuses to him.

"Are you quite alright, my dearest dæmon?" Miel suddenly asked, lowering his hand from his hair to place it against his chest instead. His fingers stroked at the neckline of his tunic, not grabbing hold of the silk exactly, but just softly stroking at it. "You seem a little... quiet this evening?"

"Yes, I am just, uh, I am just a little surprised to see you again after last night," Satariel replied, as he tried his hardest to hold his gaze. "It almost seemed like a dream to me, to meet an angel like you. But now, I am starting to realise that it was real and not fantasy."

This made Miel's lips curl up in that sweet smile of his, which made it harder to look at him. Just a flash of his teeth between his lips seemed to make him glow even more, his radiance reaching a level that made Satariel want to drop his head in awe and shame.

Miel agreed, "It almost seemed like a dream to me too; to meet a dæmon as gentle as you. One that likes to watch mortal babes playing and not eat them, and has such little horns."

Satariel looked up sharply at this, just in time to see Miel's eyes wrinkling deeply at the corners as he let out a soft laugh. The sound was as melodious as his singing was, and the sight of him reaching up to cover his mouth with his fingers brought a soft smile to his own lips.

"That does not offend you, does it? Calling them little?" Miel asked, and his expression showed slight caution, almost like he was scared that he might have upset him with his remark. "It is just that they are so awfully small, Satariel, and I quite like them."

"You... you like them?" Satariel asked in return, and he was so shocked by his words that he did not even think to answer his question.

"I do, I think they are... sweet – funny, even," he explained, before quickly adding. "Not in a mocking way; I just always thought that dæmon horns were massive, and yours are so different to what I thought that I suppose I find my assumptions the amusing part. Do you not like your horns, my dearest dæmon?"

"I do not like them because they have cut my fingers so many times, but..."

"But?"

"But it is not my horns' fault, I should not be angry at them for such a thing," Satariel finished with a soft shrug.

"I agree, you should learn to love and accept your horns,

Satariel. They are a part of you, just like my wings are a part of me, and they make you unique."

When the angelic being once more gave him that radiant smile, it made his very core almost tremble like the catkins on the pussy willow did in the gentle breeze.

"Ah, the rain has brought the beautiful scent of petrichor with it," Miel said, as he closed his eyes and took a deep inhale. "I will bet that the mortals will be happy, for this scent means cool weather again at last. You like the scent, do you not, Satariel?"

"I do, it is that earthen scent I love the most," Satariel agreed, hunkering down to sink his fingers into the soil and pull a handful free.

The dirt was cold against his skin as he sank his fingers into it, and gritty particles slipped under his nails to get trapped, just like it settled in the folds of skin on his fingers and palms. When he straightened up again, his fingers cradling a thick clod of earth, he noted that Miel was studying him with a curious expression, as if he was confused by his actions.

Satariel had to place his free hand under his fist to catch the soil that slipped free between the cracks in his fingers. The scent of the earth wafted up in wonderful waves to float around them, as aromatic as any perfume.

"Smell it," he suggested, holding his fist out to the other being. "If you breathe in deeply enough, you can detect hints of other things too. Like clay, sand, and silt. Sometimes, you can smell iron and sulfur depending on the area, and–"

"Satariel," Miel said, dragging his name out before letting out a sweet giggle. "What are you doing?"

"I am letting you smell it," Satariel replied, gently shaking his hand for emphasis.

"I can smell it just fine, you do not need to do that," he replied, smiling from ear-to-ear. "I do not need to burrow down in the soil to smell it, but…"

Miel let his words trail off into a soft mumble as he studied his dirty hands, clearly still thinking over what he wanted to say. After a moment, he decided to slightly lean forward to get closer to the soil. He hovered over his hands, taking an inhale of the scent and lifting his gaze up to look at him.

"Touch it too; you can feel all of the sensations that way," Satariel suggested, holding his gaze without reservation. "I know that you like touching things, and you said that you like standing in the wet mud."

Miel reached over to place his hand on top of his, imploring him to let him take hold of some of the soil.

Satariel took a sharp intake of breath at his sudden touch, his hands trembling so much that it was a miracle he did not drop the clod of earth on their bare feet by accident.

"Oh! Your hands are cold, my dearest dæmon," Miel exclaimed, before snagging a thick handful of the damp soil from his palm.

It was almost black in shade, the current dim dusk light sucking all the colour out of it.

But at dawn, even when it was still wet with dew, the dirt would be much more than just pitch-black. It would be rich with shades of brown and even red, should there be a concentration of clay in the soil. The range of colours could be as vibrant and fascinating as the mixtures of scents that it contained.

"Hmm," Miel softly sighed, rubbing his fingers and thumb together to feel the texture of the soil. "I can see why you like the scent of the earth so much, my dearest dæmon. It *is* more complex than I thought."

"What does it feel like to you?"

"Why do you ask?"

"Well, I told you about taste, so you should tell me about the sensations that you enjoy the most," Satariel suggested, as he also rubbed the soil between his hands to feel it. "You have got a nice way of describing things. I like listening to you talking, little angel."

Miel looked up from the soil at this, watching him rubbing at the clod of earth with a great interest before lifting his gaze to look at his face. It seemed that he was thinking of something to say to him, perhaps a way of describing the sensations that he was currently feeling. It took him a moment, but Satariel saw his features lighting up when he finally found the right words.

"Um, exquisite," Miel said, his lips once more splitting into a pleased smile. "It feels *exquisite*, Satariel. It is so cold and gritty, but it smells so pure that I almost want to rub it on my skin and feel it that way."

"Then rub it on your skin," he suggested, shooting him a wide and very mischievous grin.

"Huh?" Miel hummed, glancing up from their soiled-covered hands to hold his gaze.

Rather than repeat himself, Satariel moved to slap his hand against his own forearm so he could start rubbing the damp earth onto his skin.

For a moment, Miel just stared at him with comically wide eyes, and then he burst out laughing. The sound was as airy as his singing, and it made Satariel's core almost catch alight so that he flooded with a warmth that made him feel *good.*

"Satariel! Your skin, you are going to end up filthy!" Miel declared between his giggles, his own fingers tightening around the clod of soil in his palm. "You should not do that!"

"But it feels so wonderful," Satariel countered, still very much massaging the soil into his skin in circular motions. "You should try it too, little angel."

Miel hesitated for a moment, as he watched him coating his forearm from the delicate crease of his elbow right down to the curved bone of his wrist.

Satariel was telling him the truth – it really did feel wonderful to rub the gritty and damp earth against his skin until it smeared into a paste of some kind; a paint that he could smooth with ease. It was cold and thick, and it just felt strangely pleasant. So much so that he hunkered down to retrieve some more and started rubbing it onto his other arm.

As he massaged the earth into his skin, Satariel saw Miel finally moving to try it himself. He pressed the handful of soil against his arm first, loosening his fingers so that he could smooth it down his forearm too. In the act of doing so, a lot of the dirt sifted down in a cloud to land on their feet, but he still smeared quite the amount against his skin.

"Oh!" Miel gasped, his expression shifting into a quick

grimace before he let out a laugh. "That feels... it feels *wonderful,* Satariel!"

Satariel gave the angel a smile that said all that he needed to say – *"I told you so".*

Miel gently brought his filthy hand back up his forearm to continue smoothing at the damp soil. There was a sweet smile on the angel's face because he must have found the sensation highly pleasing.

A sudden urge came to mind as Satariel studied his own soil-covered palm, one that was so unexpected and naughty that he could not believe that he had thought of it. But as mischievous as it might just be, he still found himself giving in to the sudden impulse.

Satariel reached over the space between them to wipe his filthy hand against Miel's rosy cheek.

The sudden contact was enough to make the angel flinch, his eyes squeezing shut as a little gasp escaped him. But then he twisted to look at him, his own hand pausing in the act of massaging at his forearm.

For a moment, and just a moment, Satariel panicked and thought that he might just have done something wrong; something disrespectful and mean to the holy being. He could see the dirt all over his face, the splayed marks of his fingers like a slap right there on his hot and golden skin. But then something glinted in the blue depths of the angel's eyes, something sweet and so very naughty.

"You little devil!" Miel exclaimed, his lips cracking open in the widest smile that Satariel had ever seen on his face. "You dæmonic babe!"

"That was an exquisite sensation; wasn't it, little angel?"

When Miel moved to grab hold of his dirty elbow in his equally dirty hand, Satariel was powerless to stop him. All he could do was squirm in his grip with a series of noises that were trapped between laughter and weak gasps. He was almost enveloped by his aura of warmth and light as the angel pulled him closer, which he longed to suck up into his own body.

Miel took great delight in wiping damp dirt right across the bridge of his nose, tapping at the rounded tip playfully until he went cross-eyed following his fingers.

"Does that feel wonderful, my *naughty* dæmon?" Miel taunted, that playful glint trapped in his eyes. "It is exquisite?"

Satariel hummed in agreement and let Miel wipe even more of the earth on his cheek, just because it allowed to him stay so close to his heat and radiance.

Seeing the way that the angel's lips twitched at the corners in amusement, how pleased that he looked to be playing around with him like one of the mortal children they both loved to watch, was something that Satariel had not imagined he would have witnessed tonight.

Satariel had expected plenty of curious questions just like the previous dusk, and perhaps some soft touches here and there. He had imagined they would have found a place to perch, like the felled tree trunk that they had shared yesterday, and they would have fallen into a debate about angels and dæmons, and all other things that fascinated them.

Yet his bold and rather naughty antics had somehow managed to bridge that small divide between them, and it had brought them closer together than he had thought possible.

Miel was not hesitantly touching his horns, he was skittering his fingertips over his nose and cheeks; his touch confident and not at all shaking with trepidation.

Oh, how Satariel longed to be able to touch the angel's delicate nose and rosy cheeks without trembling in the fingers and toes too.

After a moment, Miel seemed to realise just how close that they were, and so he slowly pulled his hand away from his face. He gave him a quick smile as he did so, which Satariel managed to return, even when the corners of his lips felt rubbery.

"At dusk, when we were talking about the sensations that I enjoy, I forgot to mention a very important one. Satariel, do you ever dip your fingers and toes in the brook to clean them?"

"No, I have never done that before," Satariel lied in a soft voice. "I have never cleansed my skin in these woods."

"Well, we must cleanse ourselves now, my dearest

dæmon," Miel remarked, as he looked down at their filthy limbs with a smile. "We look so silly – like those mortal babes after they play wrestle with each other and get dirt all over their skin and leaves in their hair."

This comparison made them laugh, as it was very apt. They might not have leaves in the hair, but they had come very close to wrestling at some point, when Miel had grappled hold of him and had tugged him close like that.

"Come, Satariel, let us cleanse ourselves, hmm?"

Miel took hold of his wrist so he could pull him away from the pussy willow and across the clearing, naturally taking the lead. His fingers wrapped around his wrist with a firm, but not tight grip. It was a secure grip, one that would keep him from breaking free and possibly grabbing more dirt with which to smear all over his body. His upper arms were free from soil, Satariel noted, and the golden and supple curve of muscle was just begging to be sullied too. The temptation to reach over and touch his arm was so very powerful, but there was one urge that overruled it entirely.

Satariel hastily wiped his other hand on the front of his tunic, trying his hardest to clean it free from soil. As soon as it was as clean as it was going to get, he reached over and settled his hand right down on the curve of one of Miel's wings.

Just like last time, Miel's wings reacted to his touch by way of twitching. It was so fascinating to watch them doing so because when the muscles at the base of his shoulder blades clenched tight and then loosened, every single feather would dance from the slight movement. It made the dim, fading sunlight ripple across their surfaces, and it created even more wonderful hues for him to observe.

Satariel felt his breath leaving his lungs in a soft sigh, almost hypnotised by the myriad of colours that appeared for a mere moment before disappearing again.

A single blink would mean that he would miss the shades, and so he resumed gently stroking his fingers along his feathers in the hopes of producing more magical tones. He could sense that Miel was looking at him with curious eyes, but he was far too busy observing his wings to return his gaze.

Were bird feathers this magnificent? Of all the birds that he had caught in the past, Satariel could not recall catching one with feathers like these ones. Their soft feathers seemed dull and rough in comparison to the colourful and silken ones that he was stroking now. He wondered if all angel feathers were like this too, or if Miel was just a special angel – or perhaps, a more perfect specimen.

Miel guided him across the glen and past the small cave, dipping deeper into the woods. They had to duck below some dangling branches and stretches of thick vines to save getting tangled in their snaking hold. Within seconds, they were disappearing into the thick darkness that the copse of trees cast.

The brook ran quite the distance through the woods and right down past the village itself; but the best location to bathe their skin in was up a sloping mountain path. The many tributaries that ran off from the mountain spring were too small for use, unless they only wanted to cup a handful and sip at the crystal-clear water.

The little creatures could sip at the brook water with ease, as could the growths of wild flowers and vegetation that grew in massive bundles in the surrounding area. They just so happened to pass a creature that was watering itself at the trickling stream.

"Ah, God is good," Miel said in a soft voice, and his tone revealed that he was smiling at the sight of the deer. "This is a blessed dusk for the both of us, dearest dæmon."

Satariel could see that the deer was a doe, a fully-grown doe with a hide of vibrant copper that was dappled with splotches of white. Her legs were so thin and yet so strong, capable of propelling her up high in the air and galloping off into the trees – should she catch sight or sound of them.

As she lapped up water with her soft, pink tongue and white lips, her black eyes never once settled in place, but resumed scanning her surroundings for signs of danger.

"You really like the little creatures, do you not?" Satariel asked, as Miel slowed down to observe the deer for a moment longer.

"I love all of God's creatures – big and small. They all serve a purpose, they all have a meaning that they fulfil just by existing," Miel explained, still watching the doe as she drank her fill of brook water. "This deer, she may destroy a lot of vegetation in this forest, but her faeces sustain so many little bugs. Her meat also sustains predators, both scavenging foxes, and hunting humans and wolves. Even after death, her body will help hundreds of little creatures remain living. It is beautiful; do you not think so, my dearest dæmon?"

"A little angel that loves all the little creatures," Satariel remarked, giving the angel a sidelong smile. "I find death and putrefaction as beautiful as you do. When this doe dies, she goes into the earth, and it continues its immortal cycle. Her meat is also hot and delicious in my belly, should I choose to devour her."

"You are not... you are not going to devour her, are you?" Miel asked in a quiet voice, his grip involuntarily tightening around his wrist.

"Not in front of you, little angel."

From somewhere deep within the woods, the crisp sound of a twig snapping was enough to make the deer swing her head up. Her body fell still, almost deathly so, save for her tufted ears – which swivelled around to better track the sound. After a few seconds, she bounded off back into the underbrush, leaving them to watch her fleeing rump and twitching white tail.

Miel decided to resume their journey through the woods after this pleasant encounter, gently tugging him along the stretch of the trickling stream.

Eventually, the stream ran back into the mouth, rather than into several thin tributaries. If they so wanted to, they could have bathed their entire bodies in the wide stretch of water, for it ran deep and strong before cascading down in small waterfalls.

They had to clamber up small boulders to get to the best spot, and then Miel gently lowered himself down to sit on the edge of an overhanging chunk of rock.

Miel dipped his right foot into the water first, before letting out a surprised laugh. His toes clenched tightly to scrunch his bare foot up, deep wrinkles appearing in his skin.

"It is cold, so cold," he explained, once more dipping his toes in the water to keep them in place. "But it feels nice after you get used to it. Try it, Satariel, I am sure that you will love it too."

Satariel watched the angel kicking his foot around in the stream for a moment, and then he shifted to gently lower himself down onto the rock beside him. As he settled in place and hovered one of his filthy feet above the water, he saw the way that Miel was wriggling his toes around. The act was so endearing that it brought a smile to his face, and he finally took the plunge to dip his own foot into the stream.

"Oh!"

The cold was instantaneous, so shockingly icy, that Satariel pulled his foot straight out of the water a mere moment later. It was not like the damp soil, which was *exquisitely* cold, but like a sudden downpour of rain that soaked his hair to his scalp and drowned his poor tunic within seconds – an unpleasant kind of cold.

Maybe it was his little exclamation, or maybe it was his twitching toes, but Miel let out a giddy giggle beside him. He had lowered both of his feet down into the chill water, and he seemed to be enjoying the bracing cold. The stream water was such a clash against the waves of heat that were coming off of Miel's body that Satariel could hardly believe it.

"It is too cold, little angel! How can you stand it?!" Satariel exclaimed, droplets of water dripping down from his wet toes.

"I told you, Satariel – I love sensations," Miel explained, as he kicked his feet around in the water to produce many ripples and little bubbles. "The sudden cold makes my body shudder like no other, makes me wriggle and squirm and – oh! It is just delightful!"

Satariel thought this over for a moment, as he looked between the angel's smiling face and their feet. Then he decided to brave another dip, gently lowering his wet foot back into the stream. He swallowed a gasp of shock and clenched his fingers around the skirt of his filthy tunic, and then he added his second foot into the stream.

Miel was right – the sudden cold *did* make him want to wriggle, squirm, and whine from the discomfort. It took a moment or two, but the cold did seem to settle in a way that meant it was no longer unpleasant.

Perhaps he had adjusted to the temperature?

Or perhaps he was just simply numb to it?

Whatever the case, Satariel felt the need to chatter his teeth and wriggle lessening until he was able to let go of his tunic and relax.

"See? It feels nice, does it not?"

"Mmm, it feels nice," Satariel agreed, as he wriggled his toes in the cold stream just like he was doing so. He could see soil dissipating out into the water with every passing second; the fast stream hitting against his skin and washing all of it away. "It would be nicer if it was hot water."

"Hmm, that would warm you up, Satariel," Miel agreed with a soft nod. "You do need to keep warm; your poor hands were frozen when I touched them before. Are you always that cold?"

Satariel hummed in agreement, rather than speak, because there was so very little to say on the matter.

After some more kicking and toe-wiggling, Miel shifted to lean forward over his knees and stick his hand down into the water.

"We are like those mortal babes," he joked, as he started cupping handfuls of water into his palm so that he could clean the soil from his forearms. "With their funny games, rubbing soil all over ourselves. How silly we are."

Satariel copied his actions, even when the freezing cold water splashing against his skin made him wince. He suddenly realised just how silly his actions had been now that he had to clean the dirt free.

But in the moment... in the moment, Satariel had felt no regrets. It had been far too exciting playing with Miel in such a childish way to regret it now, and he just knew he would repeat his childish and mischievous impulses once more – if possible.

Miel used his reflection in the stream to help him wash

away the dirt on his cheek, wiping his damp hand across his skin rather than splashing the cold water on it.

"Here, Satariel, let me," Miel said, as he shifted on the rock to face him.

"Mmm?"

The angel reached over to cup his chin, turning his head towards him so that he could look at him. For a few seconds, Satariel could only stare back at him with wide eyes, his own hands dripping cold water down onto his thighs. But then the Miel lifted his other hand to brush his damp fingers down the bridge of his nose, and he suddenly understood what he was doing.

Miel was cleaning his face for him.

Miel's hands were so warm, so soft that it was unbelievable. His touch alone was enough to leave a lingering residue of heat on his skin, along with a gentle tingling that seemed to be healing.

Whilst he tenderly wiped his thumb across his cheek to clean away the dirt, Satariel could only close his eyes and track the movement. Even after Miel moved his hand away, that warmth remained on his skin; reminding him that he had been touched by a blessed being he was unworthy of even glancing upon.

"There, I think that we are all clean now," Miel said with a warm smile, his own golden skin free from a hint of soil and covered in little beads of water.

Satariel pulled his feet out of the brook to see that they were clean; but they were also a rather surprising shade of pink in parts. The cold water had chilled them through, and as a result, his toes looked chapped. The cool air of the glen was even more unpleasant, for it just added to the numbing chill.

"I cannot feel my toes," he remarked, pitifully trying to wiggle and clench them.

"The water can be very numbing," Miel agreed, pulling his own feet out of the stream to reveal that his golden toes were also pink from the chilly temperature. "I like to massage my feet afterwards to warm them up. Here."

Satariel watched Miel moving to take hold of his ankle,

and it took him a moment to realise what he was doing.

When he pulled on his ankle, Satariel allowed him to move him by turning to face the angel. His tunic shamelessly wracked up his thin thighs, just like Miel's did so when he crossed his legs in front of him. He reached down to try and fix it back in place in embarrassment, but the angel's eyes did not even glance up from his feet.

Miel did not seem to care that his silken tunic was going to get wet from his feet, for he just placed them down into the cradle of his lap and proceeded to take hold of one of his ankles so he could massage that foot first.

Satariel could feel the silk underneath his feet, stretched taut across Miel's firm thighs, and he could not help but clench his toes and wrinkle it.

Satariel could not believe that an angel, a blessed being of Heaven itself, had his feet in his lap. He could not understand why such a higher creature would lower himself so much, by willingly touching his feet like this. It should be the other way around – he should be the one cowering at his feet, showering them with kisses and begging for mercy from his divine wrath.

Yet Miel was cradling his feet in his warm lap, warming them once more as he kneaded his fingertips and thumbs into his skin, and the serene expression on the angel's face made Satariel feel so very strange.

Satariel felt small and weak in the presence of such heavenly grace, but he also felt... safe; protected, even.

He might just be a wretched dæmon, but Miel's healing aura was starting to make him feel like he might not have to be a *lonely,* wretched dæmon.

"You have got so many scratches on your skin, Satariel," Miel said in a quiet voice, his thumb tracing the aged lines in his soles. "The dirt and grass stains covered them yesterday, but now I can see them clearly. Why are they so scratched?"

"I do not know," Satariel replied with a soft shrug, avoiding his gaze to watch his fingers tracing over his foot instead. "There is a lot of sharp rocks in the ground, and I stand on them sometimes."

"Your skin... it should be calloused and tough, but it is still so soft in the parts that are not scarred," Miel remarked, eyeing the sole of his foot with a great fascination. "It must hurt terribly to stand on those sharp rocks, my dearest dæmon."

"Pain is subjective."

"I would not know, I have never felt pain before," he replied, as he stopped massaging his left foot and focused on his right foot instead. "I find your scars highly intriguing. Do they hurt? Is there a lingering sensation on your skin, or can you not feel a thing?"

"It hurts when you touch them."

Miel froze at this, his thumbs stopping in the middle of his kneading massage and his eyes lifting to stare up at him. They were rounded with shock, and his lips were parted ever so slightly.

"Not like that, little angel, not because of you," Satariel rapidly explained. "My scars hurt when I put pressure on them, or when there is a sudden, chill winter wind. The skin has long healed, but the pain still lingers. I do not know why; the scars just ache sometimes. It reminds me of how guilt often lingers, even long after a sin or a mistake has been committed."

Miel thought this over for a moment, still holding his foot between his hands but not moving to resume the massage. Then he slowly started rubbing his thumbs against the sole of his cold foot, but he did so with remarkably more tenderness than he had with his other foot; just to not press down against his scars and cause him any more aches and pains.

As soon as he was finished, Satariel folded his own legs in front of him to create a cradle in which to hold Miel's feet. The angel had not asked him to do so, nor had he vocally offered, but he just silently bade that he let him massage at his cold feet too – just like he had done so the previous dusk.

Miel shifted to unfold his legs, cocking his knees up in front of him to allowing Satariel to gently clasp hold of his ankle and move to place it down in his lap.

Unsurprisingly, Miel's skin did not feel as cold as his had felt after being in the stream. When Satariel touched his feet, he found them to be cool instead of cold, and his warmth was steadily increasing with every passing second. Soon, they would be as hot as the rest of his skin was, but that was not going to stop Satariel from massaging his feet.

"I told you about how we eat mortal hearts," Satariel said to break their momentary silence, choosing his left foot to lavish with attention first. "You told me that angels do not eat anything at all. It made me curious about your kind, and I want to know more about angels, Miel."

"I… well, its hard talking about my kind, as we do not live like dæmons do. It might sound strange, but you are closer to mortals than we are in that regard, because you sustain your existence by consuming and-and copulating."

Satariel heard the stutter in Miel's words at this, and he wondered if it was the word 'copulating' that had caused it, or the fact his thumbs might have kneaded against a sensitive spot on his sole. He looked up to see that Miel was playing with the ends of his tunic, lightly wrinkling the pink silk between his fingers as he watched him.

"We do not have a need to eat, because we are free from sin," Miel continued, his brow slightly furrowed because he was thinking about the subject so intensely. "Consuming is a weakness brought upon by sin, much like other bodily needs and urges that mortals and little creatures possess. So, I do not eat anything at all, as I have no desire to do so."

The fact that Miel's feet were free from any scarring, be it from stepping on sharp stones, or the general wear and tear that created calluses, was not surprising to Satariel. He was an angel, after all, and it made sense that his skin be as flawless as the rest of him appeared to be.

Free from sin and flaw, and also hatred.

"Can you eat though, little angel? Should you desire to do so, could you eat something?" Satariel asked, pressing his thumbs down deep into the arch of his foot and seeing Miel's toes clenching from the pressure.

"Um," Miel hummed, as he took a sharp intake of breath. "I think so? I have never wanted to eat something before, but I suppose that I *could* taste something, at least. Maybe not consume it like you can, my dearest dæmon, but at least let it settle on my tongue."

"Have you ever wondered what something tasted like?"

"A couple of times, I have wondered what it would be like to taste certain things, but I have never given in to the temptation to sample such things. Why do you ask?"

Satariel shifted his fingers up to the angel's toes, so that he could give them little touches. Not exactly strokes or squeezes, but something caught between both actions. He did not seem particularly ticklish, or at least not his feet, but that did not mean that he was not ticklish elsewhere.

"I could tell you what such things taste like, if you want? Whatever you wanted to taste, I will have tasted it before, little angel."

"Oh? Oh, um, then what does... water taste like?" Miel asked, sitting bolt upright and eyeing him with much eagerness.

This innocently naïve question made Satariel start laughing. He was unable to help himself because of all the things that Miel could have asked him... he had asked about the taste of water.

Satariel was quick to explain, "Little angel, water does not have much of a taste. Sometimes, you might detect a hint of sweetness or bitterness, depending on where you sample the water, but it mostly remains tasteless on the tongue. Even my much more sensitive tongue does not detect much flavour. But perhaps angel tongues can taste water as sweet as honey?"

"Oh, I see," Miel said in a quiet voice. "Then what about honey? What does honey taste like?"

"Honey has hundreds of flavours," Satariel replied, as he moved onto his second foot to give it a massage. "Mostly, it tastes sweet. But it has a variety of underlying flavours that can be a result of where it was harvested, and the bees that produce it. Sometimes, it is fruity, or floral, or even spicy. Do you know what those things even taste like?"

"Um..." Miel hummed, and he played with his tunic skirt in a fidgeting manner. "I know what the words mean, and I know how what those things *smell* like, so I guess that I know what they taste like too – by association. Sometimes, strong

56

fragrances linger in my mouth. Does that count?"

"Well, honey is very thick and sticky," Satariel continued, as he massaged at his smooth and warm skin. "It feels nice to suck it off your fingers and swallow it; so smooth and sweet. My favourite honey is wildflower and sourwood; they are by far the greatest. I also adore honeysuckle, but that is not exactly honey – that is nectar."

Miel was listening to him talk with rapt attention, his wings twitching every now and again so that his feathers ruffled. His lips were slack and his eyes rounded, and his hands shifted to settle on his thighs rather than fiddle with his tunic.

"Honey sounds nice, Satariel," he said, after a moment of contemplation. "Do you eat honey a lot?"

"I do, I love it," he agreed, finally relinquishing his hold on his foot and glancing up at him. "I have never been stung by a bee before; they let me steal all the honeycomb I could want. And yet, I only take a small chunk."

"That is very nice of you. I told you, you are a kindhearted little dæmon; are you not?"

Miel pulled his feet off of his lap so he could shift to get up on his knees instead. He comfortably sat down on his heels, the position highly similar to that which the mortals used when praying. When he moved to take hold of his upper arm, Satariel was taken by surprise for a moment. But then he realised what he was doing, and so he relaxed in his hold and allowed him to take hold without resistance.

Just like with their feet, Miel's fingers and thumbs gently dug into his biceps as he gave his chill arm a soothing and warming massage. He started at his biceps and slowly moved his hands down to his elbow, gently massaging as he went, before concentrating on his forearm. Upon reaching his hand, he took hold of it between the both of his.

"Hmm," Miel hummed, as he entwined their fingers and held them up. Their palms touched, their fingers lightly entwined together. His lips lifted in a sweet smile, which might just have been amusement – it was difficult to tell. "I was so shocked to see that you had fingers and toes last night, Satariel, and now I cannot seem to stop looking at and touching them. How funny."

Satariel studied his smiling face for a few seconds, and then he shifted his gaze to their entwined hands. He could feel the heat of his palm toasting at his own cool skin, and the soft squeeze of his fingers between his as they layered over the backs of his prominent knuckles.

Miel's fingers were surprisingly small: small and somewhat chubby in a way that clashed against his own long fingers. Satariel felt another sudden burst of naughtiness coursing through him.

"See, you *are* a little angel! Such cherubic hands!" Satariel exclaimed with a wicked grin, even as Miel protested against this and tried to pull his hand free. "Are all angel's hands this small, Miel? Or are you just a special angel; an especially small angel?"

"They are not small, they are just..."

Miel did not finish this, he just silently stared at their entwined hands. Was he thinking of something to say, or had he realised that there was no point in denying the fact?

"They are what, little angel? Charming?" Satariel suggested, still grinning at him as he gave his hand a squeeze.

"Do you think that they are charming?" Miel asked in a whisper, slowly lifting his eyes to hold his gaze again.

Satariel thought this over for a moment, seeing the way that the angel was looking at him with something almost expectant in his eyes. Then he decided to take hold of his other hand, and he lifted it up out of his lap so he could entwine their fingers together.

"I think that angel fingers are very charming, no matter how small or chubby they might just be," he remarked with a smile. "Just like my horns, mmm?"

This made Miel smile happily, his wings fluffing up with a soft ruffle. Satariel felt a slight breeze against his face from the movement. Ah, the angel looked so radiant when he smiled like that, and it just added to the sensation of light and heat coming from his body.

"You feel warm now, Satariel," Miel remarked, cocking his head to the side so that a lock of pink hair fell across his brow. "Earlier, you were so cold that you gave me chills just touching you. Now, your hands feel so warm. I wonder why?"

"Because of you," Satariel replied, perhaps a little more forwardly than he had been intending.

Yes, he could see from the way that Miel's eyes widened at the corners that he had been far too blunt with his words. There was intent behind them that might be too strong for their current level of mutuality, and he was frightened that he might seem desperate for attention and acceptance from the angel.

"I mean, you radiate a lot of-of heat and light, little angel," Satariel quickly stammered, feeling his grip tightening around Miel's hand as he did so. It might have reached the point of being uncomfortable, but he made no sight or sound of pain. "So much heat that I think I might be absorbing it – sucking it all up like-like a disgusting parasite."

"Parasite?" Miel repeated, his lips pouting out in something that looked like surprise.

"I cannot help it, I just feel..."

Satariel closed his eyes with a heavy sigh. He wanted to let go of Miel's hands, but the angel was holding on tight and so he was unable to do so. All he could do was listening to the babbling brook to their side, lapping over the rocks and dropping down the waterfalls with a soft roar, whilst he waited for him to say something.

When he opened his eyes a slight hint, glancing at Miel through his thick eyelashes, Satariel saw that he was studying their entwined hands with a great interest. He slowly brushed his thumb across the bump of his knuckles, the contact as warm and soothing as it had been against his scarred feet.

"My dearest dæmon, you are not a parasite," Miel declared, and he brought his shoulders up in an attempt at looking confident. "You are no more a parasite than... than a flower is for sucking up the rain when it soaks into the soil. If I radiate such warmth, I must not need it, and so you should happily absorb it."

When Miel brought their hands up to his face, Satariel could do no more than stare at him. He was unable to speak, to say a thing in reply to this, because the angel had caught him by complete surprise. He had once more shown a level of selfless compassion and acceptance that he did not feel he deserved.

"Hmm, I can still smell the soil on your skin," Miel said in a soft voice. His breath was warm against his knuckles, and so Satariel felt his fingers twitching in his hold. "It is still so strong, I almost imagine that the scent will cling to you forever. But there is something else too, something similar, but..."

Miel's voice trailed off at this, his expression shifting as he stared at his nails. It seemed like he had finally noticed the thread of red that was trapped underneath them; that rusty and deep red stain that water was never able to wash free.

"Satariel, is that...?"

"I ate a heart today," Satariel explained in a quiet voice. He turned his head to stare at the rushing stream because he was too ashamed and scared to look at the angel. "It was a mortal that owed me a great reward, and so I claimed it this very dawn. The smell of it never goes away, it lingers under my nails and on my skin – I can never be free from it."

"It is fascinating," Miel said in a whisper-soft voice, as he held his hand right in front of his face. "Satariel, blood smells just like... like the earth to me. It is rich, it is coppery, it contains so many layers of... of nutrients. You told me that you love the scent of the earth because the earth is immortal. Do you love the scent of blood too?"

"No," he replied in his own whisper, the word slipping free so softly that he did not even know if the angel had heard him.

"Hmm?"

"I said no – no, I do not. I do not like the scent of blood, Miel. It is a deadly scent for me because it makes me hunger for more; more blood, more hearts, more slain mortals. Blood is like a drug for me, but it is a drug that I need to survive. I must have it. Believe me, little angel, when I tell you that I tried so hard to resist it in the past. But I *need* it, you understand?"

"Satariel, you tried to... to resist eating hearts?" Miel asked in shock, his fingers involuntarily tightening around his to squeeze his knuckles. "Why would you do such a thing?"

60

"Because I hate it, Miel!" Satariel cried out in exasperation, tugging his hands out of his so he could turn away from the angel. He pulled his legs up in front of him and dropped his face to his knees, longing to just shrivel up and disappear from his crippling self-disgust. "I hate existing like this – always hungry, always cold and weak. I wanted to-to try and resist the temptation to eat hearts, just to see if I could.

"But I went rabid from the hunger, Miel, and I attacked many mortals to fill that hideous hollow inside of me. I-I dined on hearts and flesh! Do you understand? I gorged on mortal meat until I made myself sick, and then I went mad with anger and disgust!"

"... Oh, Satariel," Miel sighed, his voice uneven and breathless.

"I have never felt pain like the pain that I felt going hungry, and then I felt even more pain from my guilt," Satariel moaned, reaching up to touch his horns just so he could hold onto them. It often felt comforting to hold onto his horns, even at the risk of slicing his skin to ribbons. "I hate being like this, Miel!"

As Satariel gently rocked back and forth, Miel reached over to place his hand on his back. He settled it in place for a moment, before gently shifting it up to his shoulder to give it a comforting squeeze.

"When we were watching that deer, you said something, little angel. You said that all creatures serve a purpose and have a meaning for their existence. Do I have a purpose? Do I have meaning?"

Satariel lifted his head up off his knees so he could look at him, blinking hard in an attempt at forcing away the stinging tears at the corners of his eyes.

"You do have a purpose," Miel replied, as he gave his shoulder another firm squeeze. "You are a dæmon, Satariel, and that is not a bad thing. You exist with a purpose, even if that purpose is... ungodly. If you had no reason to exist, then you would not. No dæmon would exist, but the fact you do means that you have a purpose in this world. It is hard to understand these things, because we are not like the little creatures. We have a profound understanding of existence, and with that understanding comes doubt, fear, and denial."

The angel paused for a moment to let this sink in, before continuing. "But I think that you exist with a meaning, Satariel. It might just be that meaning was to meet me. Maybe we exist solely to meet one another? You have touched upon me in an irrevocable way, and that alone has made you worthy of existence."

"Do you... do you think so, little angel?"

"I know so, my dearest dæmon," Miel agreed, and he moved his hand to cup his face just in time to wipe a single tear away from his cheek with his thumb. "Now, about tastes. If honey can have so many different tastes, then does that mean flowers also taste differently? Do flowers have a taste? Ah! What flowers taste the nicest, Satariel! I must know because..."

III

Just like he had thought last night, Miel was to find that the heavy rainfall had brought cooler weather with it.

Standing within the forest, a lot of the heat was still trapped by the canopies of the taller trees, along with the moisture. But he savoured the sensation greatly. The heat and moisture brought the scent of damp soil and greenery with it, which he loved breathing in as he made his way along the natural paths in the woods.

Oh, how Miel adored the powerful aroma of the earth. Much like Satariel, who loved the hints of decay trapped within the grit and mud, he found the scent calming. It was likely because the scent of the earth reminded him of his walks through the forest, and his peaceful meditation as he did so.

Wherever Satariel retired to slumber (should dæmons sleep like other beings) Miel hoped he could breathe in that scent too. He hoped that he sank down into the softest, warmest soil and slumbered peacefully – just because he loved the earth so much. The dæmon might slumber in a bed of flowers for all he knew, considering the powerful scent of gardenias that emanated from him.

But Miel could so vividly imagine him curling up within a trunk of a tree, one of the pussy willows perhaps – hidden from view and danger, and comfortable in his own little den.

At dawn, the dew was still fresh on the grass and leaves. This meant that his feet were coated with water and chlorophyll from the damp grass, as he was walking along the path with purpose, rather than lightly skipping his feet over the ground.

Miel *wanted* to dirty his soles, not only because he enjoyed the sensation of the cold beads of dew and the scent that it would leave behind, but because he might get to once more soak his feet in the stream with Satariel at dusk.

It was a long time until dusk, and there were so many things that he needed to do, but Miel was still eagerly awaiting the sunset. He had completed as many of his Heavenly duties as possible so he had been able to sneak down to the earthen plane at dawn. His plan was to return to the kingdom after tending to the shrine, undertaking his duties once more only to return at dusk to solely spend time with his dæmon companion.

If Satariel was hiding away in the trees like the previous dusk, to watch him tending to the shrine from a safe shadowy spot, then there was nothing stopping them from talking to one another. It was amusing how the dæmon had been so eager to see him again, but he had been too nervous – or or frightened – to step out from the trees and greet him.

Just thinking about how round Satariel's eyes had been when he had finally emerged from the copse of trees, his messy hair strewn across his brow and his fingers twitching at his sides, brought a fond smile to Miel's face.

"Ah, it is so mild today; is it not?" he asked, as he glanced up at the tree branches above him with that smile on his face.

The dappled crested lark just continued tweeting within the foliage of the tree, his sweet song echoing off the other trees and making Miel hum contentedly.

Yes, Satariel had seemed nervous at first, but the sensation had quickly passed. That naughty streak of his had emerged so unexpectedly, as had his unusual quirks – like massaging dirt into his skin. He was such a fascinating little dæmon that Miel was quite simply captivated by him in a way that he did not truly understand. He just needed to spend more time in his company and learn more about not only his kind, but about him too.

Satariel might just be a dæmon, but he was also a unique being. He was a being that devoured mortal hearts after entering pacts with them, and he feasted upon the meat of little creatures; but he was also a being that despised existing in such a wretched manner. It was inconceivable, and yet he had sensed complete sincerity in the dæmon's words when he had told him such a thing.

Miel would not have thought it possible for a dæmon to feel guilt for existing, but Satariel did. It was not his fault that he had to kill mortals and other creature to live because that was his design, but he seemed to carry around a burden of remorse.

Miel did not know what such an emotion felt like, as he was incapable of feeling guilt. He could only assume that it was a painful burden to carry.

All Miel could hope was that by talking to Satariel some more, he would be able to help him understand that he was a part of God's plan too. He could only pray that he helped the dæmon find guidance and acceptance, and that he understood his purpose for existence too.

Miel was starting to understand that dæmons were not as evil as he had once ignorantly assumed, and that their existence was just as necessary as his own kind were. He might not currently understand the full reasons. But he was an intelligent angel, and with enough contemplation, he knew that he would be able to come to a conclusion.

Everything that existed was so because of God, after all.

Through the gaps in the trees above him, Miel could see a sky washed with golden clouds that signalled that the day was going to be cool and bright. The stars were still fading out in the early dawn light, which meant he could see them scattered across the lilac sky. He would be able to see the moon too, should he spot it through the chinks in the thick foliage.

It was wonderful looking up at the sky, but he much preferred keeping his gaze low to look at the path in front of him.

Dust motes danced in the strong beams of light, as did tiny gnats that liked to dart around his head. They buzzed softly but never landed on his skin to bite, and so he was able to walk through their noisy clouds without a single worry. Save for the birds, the bugs were the only little creatures that he could see right now – and little they were. Such tiny beings, yet so perfect in their existence and form.

If Satariel could see how even these tiny creatures had a place in God's design, then maybe he would be able to find his own meaning too?

When Miel ducked underneath the low-hanging tree

branches to finally step into the glen, the sight of Satariel already present was not something that he had imagined he would see.

Miel stopped in complete surprise to look at him, watching the dæmon slowly crawling through a patch of flowers with his behind curved up high in the air and his head held low.

Satariel was focused on a black and blue butterfly that was settled on a fluffy bundle of white petals. Her thin wings beat softly as she presumably sampled the pollen. As he watched him, the dæmon lifted one hand to reach towards the insect as slowly as he could so that he did not scare her away with any sudden movements.

Before Miel could even blink, Satariel snatched the butterfly right from the flower and clapped his hand against his mouth.

"Satariel! No! Do not eat her!" Miel cried out, just as the dæmon was about to suck the butterfly right into his mouth.

Satariel looked up sharply at his exclamation. The insect was trapped between his lips and struggling to free herself from the fate of being crushed by his gnashing teeth.

Miel raced across the clearing to get to him, and he hunkered down and seized hold of his head to angle his face before attempting to pull the butterfly free. It was difficult to do so, on account of the fact that her wings were stuck to his wet lips. But he managed to free the poor creature and get her into the palm of his hand.

"Why did you stop me?" Satariel asked, as he reached up to touch his lips with his fingers. "I wanted to eat her."

"Why would you *eat* such a blessed creature?" Miel asked, gently enclosing his fingers around the butterfly so that she was trapped in a cage of flesh. "She is a butterfly, Satariel, not a soul or mortal heart. Look at how tiny she is, how fragile! Why?"

Satariel was quick to argue, "Well, such a tiny and fragile creature is just *demanding* to be eaten. Hunters consume weak prey, little angel, and butterflies are as weak as they come."

"It might be easy to crush and consume such tiny creatures, but is it worth it?" Miel asked, cradling the butterfly in

66

his hands and watching her beating her paper-thin wings lazily through the gaps in his fingers. "Do you feel strong consuming their insignificant bodies?"

"Strong? No, but they taste nice," Satariel stated, as he moved closer to him and bent forward to watch the butterfly with a great fascination.

"Taste? Ah, it is always about taste with you, Satariel!" he argued with a heavy sigh, his shoulders rising and falling in a hard wave. "I have never tasted a single thing, and yet you taste everything!"

"They are sweet. Sweet things are the nicest-tasting things to some, especially mortals. I like spicy things, but sweet is always good."

"Sweet? Butterflies taste sweet?" Miel asked, his brow furrowing in confusion as he looked between his hands and the dæmon.

When the word 'sweet' was said aloud, it conjured to Miel's mind images of things like: fruit, with ripe and colourful skin and juicy flesh that would melt on the tongue; honey, viscous and golden, a wonder of nature herself; or pure water coursing from cracks in rocks, which would soothe the body and soul.

These were things that smelled sweet to him, and Satariel had told him tasted that way.

Miel had never imagined things like meat, like living creatures' flesh and bones, could be sweet. Yet Satariel was now telling him that butterflies were very sweet.

Was there a chance that Satariel tasted things differently, on account of his nature? Or did Miel just not understand taste because to understand something, one needed to experience it? There was not really a scent to butterflies, and so he really could not try and ascertain how one would taste.

"Mmm, sweet like sugar on my tongue," Satariel sighed out, said tongue slipping free to lick at his lips. "It is the pollen, I think; all gathered on their bodies and inside of them – so sweet, like nectar."

Miel thought this over for a moment as he studied him,

as fascinated as always by Satariel.

The dæmon managed to make the slightest action seem grand to him, even when he never acted in a way that demanded attention. He spoke in a soft and deep voice, hardly ever gestured with his hands, and yet somehow every single movement of his arrested his very concentration.

When Miel lifted his hand so that they could look at the butterfly, it was of no surprise that she did not fly away. No, the butterfly was a mess, a crumpled ruination sitting in the gentle cradle of his palm and fingers.

"You broke her wing," Miel said in a soft voice, seeing her left wing weakly beating against the curved shield of his fingers – broken and useless. "She is as good as dead now. A butterfly lives for just mere days, and she is crippled before she can fulfil that tiny amount of life."

When he looked at Satariel, the dæmon at least had the decency to look apologetic for his actions. Even when there was no need for him to do so, he had done so just for him. He studied the insect and then dropped his head to look at his bare and filthy knees, his hair falling over his dark eyes. He reached up to give one of his small horns a little tug, and Miel could see that his lips were softly pouted out in a fashion that might just have been childish upset – spoilt and grumpy.

Miel held his hand out to the dæmon, silently bidding that he take the butterfly out of his hand and eat her. He wanted him to end the little creature's suffering because he knew that the butterfly could feel the pain that she was in – she just could not *understand* it.

Satariel glanced between the insect and his face for a few seconds, and then he moved to pick up the butterfly. He lifted the butterfly to his lips once more, sucking most of her body and her ruined wing into his mouth. With a single bite, he severed her from her good wing, and then he ended her suffering with his grinding teeth.

Miel tried to ignore the soft crunching sound that his teeth made when he chewed and swallowed the creature.

"Do you want to taste it?" Satariel asked, holding the good butterfly wing out to him in offering.

Miel studied the wing for a few seconds before lifting his gaze to look at the dæmon, and he could see nothing but complete sincerity on his features.

Satariel had not offered him it as a taunt; some horrible, twisted joke that only he would find amusing. He had offered him the wing because he genuinely thought that he might want to *taste* the creature, as absurd as that might just sound.

Miel did not *want* to taste the butterfly, as she had not needed to die so pointlessly like that. She was a blessed but ignorant creature, just like most of the ones that covered the earth. She should not have been crushed and chewed up into nothingness by Satariel's sharp, little teeth. But it was too late for such emotions when she was dead now, so he should just forget about the tiny tragedy and move on.

But... Miel found a little part of him wanting to taste the insect, even when he did not understand why.

It was likely curiosity and nothing more than that, stirred up by Satariel and his constant enticing words and actions that made him want to do such things too.

"No, Satariel, I do not wish to eat the butterfly," he replied with a soft head shake. "You eat her."

Satariel thought this over for a moment, and then he shoved the wing into his mouth and eagerly chewed it.

Butterflies might just taste sweet to the dæmon, but he did not look to have enjoyed the taste because of him. It was not his fault that he liked eating little creatures, and so Miel felt cruel for looking upon him with harsh judgement.

"What are you doing here in the woods this dawn, little angel?"

"I came to the woods to tend to the shrine," he explained, as he watched him gnawing on the remains of the butterfly. "I thought that if I tended to it at dawn I could return in the dusk and perhaps... spend more time with you."

Satariel swallowed the butterfly and then stuck his tongue out to lick at his lips, as if he was chasing any hint of flavour that might just linger on them. His eyes were rounded with something that looked like interest, the black irises reflecting the soft, dawn sunlight back at him.

"I mean, I spent a great deal of time in the pastures this morning – praying and offering guidance to the mortals," Miel clarified, as he shifted to sit down on his heels and fixed his tunic skirt in place. "My duties are never-ending, but even I must find some peace to meditate and praise God; free from the burdens of suffering and salvation."

"It sounds like your duties are burdensome, little angel," Satariel remarked, dropping to sit in the grass with a soft *thump* and folding his filthy legs in front of him. "Are they?"

"No, not like that, Satariel," he replied with a soft head shake. "My body and spirit are more than capable of fulfilling all that is required of me, but I think that... well, I *think* too much. Sometimes, I cannot seem to stop thinking, and so I need to meditate on my own and find guidance."

Satariel was quick to point out, "There is nothing wrong with thinking, little angel. It is not a sin. Thought is a sign of enlightenment, and angels are certainly enlightened beings."

Miel contemplated his words for a moment, as he watched Satariel brushing away blades of grass that were clinging to his bare knees and elbows. He did have a point, there was nothing wrong or sinful with thinking; but sometimes, he could not help but feel that his thoughts might just border on being so.

Was trying to find a way to fit dæmons, unholy and ungodly, into God's design a sinful thing to contemplate? His brothers and sisters might just think it so, but they were not all as deep thinkers as he was.

But Miel had been created perfectly, and to question his own desire to question existence and meaning would be to believe himself to be imperfect. Therefore, he should just understand and accept his want to question such matters. He had been blessed with such an ability to think, and not cursed.

"What are you doing here this early in the morn, my dearest dæmon?" Miel asked, just to force his mind away from thoughts about being imperfect or sinful.

"Butterfly catching," Satariel retorted without missing a beat, giving him a quick smile.

"Oh, was that your first butterfly?"

"Yes, they are very quick, I do not catch many. One dawn, I managed to catch *three* butterflies, and my tongue and belly were very pleased," he declared, the smile growing on his face as he hastily rubbed grass free from his skin. "Do not worry, little angel, I do not eat very many butterflies."

"You do not need to explain or defend yourself, Satariel. I should not have gotten so upset over the butterfly, seeing as I know that you eat flesh and such. I was just surprised, I think, and so, I shouted at you. My dearest dæmon, I am sorry; you can eat as many butterflies as you desire."

"Mmm, there you go – apologising to a dæmon again."

Miel returned the smile because he had once again said sorry to the dæmon over such a slight and harmless thing. It just felt right to apologise to him, even if there was not much offence in his words.

"Have you... eaten a heart today, Satariel?" he asked, reaching over to pluck a stray blade of grass out of his messy hair for him. "I cannot smell anything like blood coming from you, just fresh gardenias and dry earth."

"No, I can stay full on a single heart for months at a time, little angel," Satariel explained. "I store it in my belly, breaking it down slowly as I dine on other things to sate my ravenous hunger. Dæmons are always hungry, and so we learn to withstand the pain and savour hearts for as long as we can."

"You do? That is fascinating, Satariel," Miel said in awe, gently twirling the blade of grass between his fingers.

"Mmm, I scavenge carrion and fruits mostly," he continued, as he reached down within his tunic to pull something free.

In the act of doing so, Satariel pulled down on the front of the tunic considerably, flashing a hint of his lightly tanned skin and prominent clavicle to him. Miel saw a leather thong around his neck, on which a perfectly tapered and glossy pink flight feather of his was currently attached. However, that was not what he was retrieving.

No, Satariel pulled a small pouch free that he was also dangling around his neck, which was pulled tight with a string and looked to be bulging with goods. He unknotted the small leather pouch, revealing that it was filled with bite-sized morsels: dozens of nuts, fresh flower heads, beetles, and even a couple of fat and almost black berries.

"I fill this up with whatever I can find, just in case," Satariel explained, as he plucked one of the weakly scurrying and confused beetles from the pouch and popped it into his mouth. Just like the butterfly, it crunched between his back teeth several times as he carried on talking. "These are just little bites, but they help keep me content."

"You eat all of the time, but your body is so lean, so small," Miel remarked in a soft voice, reaching over to touch his filthy, bony knee whilst Satariel sucked a berry from his fingers. When he bit into it, a sweet scent wafted over to his nose. "It is strange, Satariel."

"I must be small, it helps me stay quick and nimble," the dæmon explained, swallowing the mouthful of berry juice. "I could not catch many butterflies if I was big now; could I?"

"No, you could not," he agreed with a soft smile, as he gave his bare knee a soft stroke and then moved his hand away. "Being small has its benefits."

Miel watched Satariel selecting another few things from his pouch: a couple of reddish-coloured nuts, which he tossed into his mouth and crunched into tiny pieces. Then he grabbed a flower head that he placed onto his knee for later consumption.

"Satariel, I... I wish to try tasting things just like you," Miel confided in a whisper, as he played with the neckline of his tunic. "Not flesh and blood, like what you enjoy, but... other things. Things like honey, and water, and sweetness. Can I?"

"Can you?" Satariel repeated, as he pulled his fingers away from his mouth and swallowed the nutty mixture. "You can do whatever you wish, little angel. Why do you ask as if it is a sin?"

But all Miel could do was shrug at the question, as he did not know. It was likely because he had never done such a thing before, and he was therefore frightened of the mere thought.

There was nothing to truly be scared about, but much

like meeting Satariel for the first time, new experiences were something that he both adored, and feared.

Satariel picked the flower head up off his knee and held it out to him in offering. "Here."

Miel accepted it from him and held it in his own hand to study it.

The flower head was a soft and milky purple shade, with four lightly curled petals and a tiny, yellow centre. It was still so fresh that the petals looked soft and smooth, rather than wrinkled and dry. The scent that came from it was powdery sweet. He deduced from the scent and sight that the flower was a lilac, which he had seen nestled within other flora in the woods.

"What do I do, Satariel? Do I just... chew on it?" Miel asked, hovering the flower in front of his lower face to sniff at it curiously.

Satariel made a noise in agreement as he shifted onto his knees, leaning close and watching him with those rounded, black eyes of his. The level of attention should have been unnerving in some way, should have made him get embarrassed, but Miel just picked the flower out of his palm and gently placed it in his mouth.

The weight was only slight on his tongue, a feather-softness that was fitting considering the thinness of the petals. When he brought his teeth together and bit down on the flower head, liquid leaked free to settle on his tongue, and it mixed with his saliva to flood his mouth with a surprising flavour.

"It... it does not taste like what it smells like, Satariel!" Miel exclaimed, reaching up to cover his mouth as he stopped chewing and let the liquid soak into his taste buds.

"What does it taste like, little angel?"

"Um, it is sweet, but there is a... a tartness behind it. It reminds me of citrus fruit scents, like... like–"

"*Lemons!*" they said in unison, before Miel let out a giggle and pressed his hand against his mouth.

"It tastes like this flower should be... yellow, instead of purple," he explained, and he cheeked the remains of the flower as he swallowed the mouthful of saliva. "The colour, the scent, the taste – they are all different, I never would have imagined that so many different things could exist in one flower!"

"Now you understand why taste is such a fascinating sense, Miel," Satariel said with a smile, watching him chewing and then swallowing the lilac. "It defies sight and scent, which means that it is always exciting."

"Oh, now that I have tasted one flower, I want to taste them *all*, Satariel!"

"There is more where that came from, little angel," Satariel said with a wicked grin. He shifted to get his feet underneath him and shoved the pouch back down the front of his tunic. "I know the *best* places to find flowers in these woods; to find *everything* that you would want to taste!"

"You do?"

Rather than reply to this, Satariel stood up and held his hand out to him.

Miel eyed his hand to see grassy, green smears on the heel of his palm and some fingertips, along with deep red stains from the berries that he had snacked upon. Then he reached up to accept his hand, allowing the dæmon to pull him to his feet and entwine their fingers together tight. His hand was cold against his, but with time, it would warm up to a nice heat because of him.

When Satariel took the lead, there was something close to a skip in his step as he pulled him along behind him across the wide clearing. He darted into the copse of trees that the pussy willow was nestled in, tugging him into a section of the woods that Miel had never wandered through – or at least not too deeply.

As a result of the thick and tall trees, the soil beneath their feet was dry and crisp, rather than cold and wet – even after the heavy rainfall. Scant sunlight came through the canopies, bleeding through the heavy foliage so that it was coloured a vivid green that plunged their skin into shades of jade or moss, depending on the strength of the sunlight.

Satariel's black hair was no longer a vague shade of blue, but reflected a myriad of green back at Miel's eyes. Much like his irises would – should he gaze back over his shoulder at him.

Miel could not help but wonder what his own hair would look like in the current forest darkness, and his wings.

Would they also reflect the green hue from the sunlight, mingling into new shades and colours? Or would they stay the same, glowing with an intense colour that could not be muted or altered?

The forest path that they traversed was wilder than his favoured path through the woods, for it was covered in snaking roots, thick tendrils of vines, and sharp rocks.

Miel tentatively stepped down for fear that he would hurt his bare soles, but Satariel almost stomped down without fear. Perhaps he knew the path as well as Miel had memorised his own favourite path. But it could also be because his feet were tough in parts from his scars, and so he had no reason to fear hurting them.

Whatever the case, after a moment of happily skipping along the path, they stumbled across a sudden obstacle. It was enough to bring Satariel to a stop, and he gazed up at the tall and impressive oak that was lying right across their path.

There was an obvious crawl space underneath the trunk that Satariel could squeeze under with ease, should he be alone. The dæmon could also scale it like a lizard, or even just go around the obstacle by walking either length of the collapsed tree.

Satariel eyed the trunk intently, trying to locate any small niches in which he could shove his fingers and use to clamber over the top of it. He clearly did not want to crawl under it on his belly like a snake. Maybe because he would get covered in dirt, or maybe because he did not want to do such a lowly thing in his presence.

But before he could find any suitable niches, Miel moved to stand behind him and slipped his arms around his thin waist to hold onto him.

"Allow me, my dearest dæmon," he whispered against his ear with a mischievous grin.

With a hard beat of his wings, Miel lifted them both up

into the air so they could soar over the felled trunk. He felt Satariel stiffening in his hold from the sudden sensation, his legs limply dangling and their feet bumping together. His hands snagged hold of his arms to hold on crushingly tight.

A breathy noise escaped him that might just have been a gasp, and his nails dug into his skin as they flew over the wide tree trunk and then descended.

When they settled back down in the grass on the other side, Miel let go of him, and Satariel swooned to land on his knees with a weak cry. The sudden collapse caught him by surprise, made him gasp and tense his wings as he stared down at him. "Oh! Are you alright, Satariel?!"

"Ah, Miel! My heart, it felt so strange!" Satariel exclaimed, grabbing hold of the front of his tunic as he took a sharp intake of air. "It soared so high, I thought it would shoot right out of my mouth!"

Miel could not help but giggle at this, as he held his hand out to him in offering to pull him back to his feet.

Satariel was perfectly fine, just a little unsteady on his feet because the sudden shift from being on the ground to being in the air had caught him by total surprise. The poor dæmon had never felt such a thing before, and it was no wonder that it had made his knees buckle like that.

"I envy your wings, but I do not envy that sensation," he remarked, as he let him help him up and then shifted to lean against him for support. "Did it feel so powerful when you first took to the air?"

"It felt wonderful, Satariel," Miel replied, looking down at him with a soft smile. "I am meant to fly, so I did not feel dizzy or weak. What would it be like if dæmons could fly, hmm?"

Satariel let out a breathless laugh at this, as he straightened up and found his feet once more. There was a flush of colour in his cheeks that showed he had found the brief flight as exciting as it had been frightening, and there was something in his black eyes that said he might just want to experience it again.

As soon as he was steady on his feet, Satariel took hold of his hand and resumed guiding him along the forest path.

There were still some treacherous obstacles underfoot, but there were no more felled tree trunks to worry about.

They were drawing close to a break in the trees when Miel noticed sudden movement out the corner of his eye, and so he turned his head to track it. "Ah! Satariel, look!" he gasped, and he came to a stop so that their entwined hands tugged hard and made the dæmon slow down. His cry was barely a whisper, even when he had no need to worry about the creatures hearing him. "Can you see them?!"

There was a kindle of hares situated underneath a rotted-out tree hollow, all huddled together for warmth.

They were a mixture of brown mostly, speckled with patches of grey and black all over their luxurious pelts. They had massive, honeyed eyes and twitching, white noses and whiskers that Miel thought were breathtakingly beautiful.

"Ah, they are so soft; are they not?" Miel remarked, studying the hares with a warm smile. "What do you think about hares, my dearest dæmon?"

"Hares are... I do not eat a lot of them," Satariel explained in a quiet voice. "I scavenge meat mostly, like deer or cattle. I do not often find hare remains worth eating, and their meat is only enjoyable when fresh and still succulent with blood from being chased. Once they grow cold, they are too tough and bitter, so I leave them be."

Miel said, "So, you leave the hares to continue their existence and sustain other little creatures. That is very kind of you, Satariel."

For some reason, this made Satariel snort soft laughter as they studied the hares; his hand held securely between his own.

As soon as Miel had drank his fill, he let Satariel carry on tugging him along the path away from the hares, and he was once more thankful for this wonderful dawn blessing.

The best spread of flowers that Satariel had brought him to was situated in a massive clearing in the forest. It was so open that the dawn sky was on perfect display, rather than hidden through the canopies, and this meant the flower beds were able to bathe in the sunlight all day long and grow vibrant, tall, and strong. They were also able to soak up as much rainfall as they could, sharing the plentiful downfall with one another in loving harmony.

Just looking out across the colourful array of flowers made Miel let his breath out in the softest of sighs.

It was beautiful, so beautiful; the splashes of colour running out all around them – pinks, oranges, reds, purples, yellows, and white of all shades imaginable blending together. He saw petals of many shapes, and blooms as tiny, wide, and large as could be. The flowers attracted a great variety of bugs, which were zipping and floating around the clearing to sample the many kinds of pollen.

"Oh, Satariel," he sighed, as he lifted his hands up and clasped them underneath his chin. "God is good! Look at all of these flowers! It is so beautiful!"

Satariel moved to step out from the trees first, stepping straight into the flower patch so he could hunker down and start plucking some free. He did so very carefully, ensuring to not trod down on any of the flowers and destroy them with reckless abandon.

Miel moved to join him in the patch, also taking careful steps as he ran his gaze over the countless blooms.

An unusual flower caught his eye, a thin white trumpet-shaped bloom that was nestled in a growth of thick green leaves and vines. He moved over to the patch and hunkered down to pluck one of them free, lifting it to his face so he could try and scent its perfume.

"Ah! No, no, no – not that flower," Satariel exclaimed, as he shifted to pluck it free from his fingers. "Jimsonweed is toxic, little angel, and though you might not die, I do not think that you want to sample it."

"It is toxic? But it looks so pretty, Satariel."

"The pretty things often are the most toxic of them all," Satariel replied, caressing the flower down his cheek and making him smile. "Let me select some flowers for you, mmm?"

"That would be very kind of you, my dearest dæmon," Miel said, and he shifted to sit down in a patch of grass and tucked his knees up in front of him. "You are the expert in taste, after all."

Satariel took this suggestion very seriously, Miel was to find. Upon him requesting that he select flowers for him, the dæmon leapt to his feet and twisted to look around the clearing; hoping to locate something of interest. He dropped the toxic jimsonweed without a single care, and then he delicately skipped through the patches of flowers to start collecting some.

Miel found it so endearing to watch him, because Satariel was so focused on finding flowers for him. He nibbled here and there on petals to sample them, slapping his tongue around his mouth as he chased after flavours to try to find the best choices.

Sometimes, this resulted in him plucking another flower free. But other times, he ended up grimacing and moving away – clearly disliking that particular taste.

For an avid butterfly catcher, Satariel made no move to snatch any from the air and eat them. Why, he hunkered down beside the colourful insects and sampled the flowers just like they were doing. The concentration on his face was noticeable, particularly in the way that he pouted his lips out and barely even blinked.

"I have found you some fascinating flavours, little angel!" Satariel declared, as he finally shifted to sit down beside him and dropped the flowers in the skirt of his tunic. There was a great variety of colours and kinds in his lap; their scents mingling into a floral bouquet. "I think that you will love these!"

The way that the dapples of golden sunlight landed down on Satariel's face, no longer tinged green from the leaves, was absolutely magical to Miel's eyes. It played off his lightly tanned skin in a way that made him glow, even if only temporarily; in a way that seemed to hint he was sucking up all the heat from every single ray of sunshine. He sorted through the flowers to neaten them out, his filthy fingers now coated in pollen and even more smears of chlorophyll.

"Here," Satariel said, as he held out the first flower to him. "I think that you will find this flower highly pleasing."

Miel accepted the flower from him, already knowing what it was because it was unmistakable even at a glance.

The flower was a carnation, with a head of thin and crinkle-edged petals that layered over and over to create a massive and tightly bloomed head. It was a deep and rich shade of hot pink at the centre, which bled out in a gradient until the petals were mostly a wonderful shade of milky pink. Overall, it was a beautiful flower, and Miel instinctively lifted it up to his nose to breathe in its scent.

Unlike the lilac that Satariel had first given him, this one did not smell powdery, or even sweet at all, but was shockingly spicy to his nose.

"Now, what does this smell like, little angel?" Satariel asked, cocking his elbows on his thighs so he could hold his head in his hands and observe him.

"I think that it smells spicy," Miel replied, before taking another soft and deep inhale of its perfume. "Hmm, not a powerful spiciness, but a pleasing one. My nose itches somewhat, makes me want to-to—"

Miel blinked rapidly before the most sudden sneeze hit him, catching him by such surprise that he was unable to even twist away or cover his face. All he could do was take a quick gasp of air and then sneeze right in the poor dæmon's face, his breath leaving him again in a high-pitched squeak.

Satariel's eyes grew round at the sudden sound, before he squeezed them shut again in surprise. The sneeze disturbed his hair, knocking a lock free from his brow before it settled back in place again.

For a few seconds, the clearing was silent save for the tweeting of distant songbirds.

"Oh! I am sorry!" Miel cried out, clapping his hand against his nose, even when he had just sneezed and it was pointless.

But Satariel was too busy laughing at his sneeze to seem to care. His shoulders were rising and falling with each guffaw as he rolled his head back and flashed his sharp teeth at him.

Miel lowered his hand from his face as he looked at him, and he wriggled his nose from side to side to chase away any hints of pollen, just to ensure he would not sneeze again.

Hopefully, the taste of the flower would not also make him sneeze, because he did not want to spit a mouthful of chewed-up petals into the poor dæmon's face.

"Yes, it must be spicy!" Satariel remarked with a smile, dropping his gaze to look at the flowers before looking up at him. "But what about the taste, mmm?"

Miel eyed the carnation again, and then he lifted it to his face to take another cautious sniff. He could still scent the spicy undertones in the perfume, but it did not make him sneeze again. He opened his lips and shoved the flower into his mouth so that he could bite the head free from the stem and chew it.

"This tastes... this is what I think sweetness tastes like," Miel explained, as he eyed the stem and chewed the mouthful of petals. "It is sweet, but not overly sweet – mild, I suppose?"

Satariel collected his own carnation so he could bite the head off it and also savour the taste. He could no doubt taste the sugary sweetness that the pollen produced when chewed up with their saliva, which was at complete odds with the spicy aroma.

"Am I right, Satariel?"

"You are indeed, little angel," he agreed, and he tossed the ruined stem aside and swallowed the mouthful of carnation.

Satariel glanced at his little bouquet once more, eyeing his choices before selecting the next two flowers from his lap.

Miel could see they were chrysanthemums of orange, though he knew they could come in many different colours.

Much like the carnations, these flower heads were tightly bloomed at the centre before layering out; but the petals were long and pointed, rather than crinkled and rounded. They were coloured the same way, with the orange deep and vibrant in the centre and then bleeding out to a creamy shade for the petals.

The chrysanthemum smelled just like the earth in a way, blended with a grassy scent so there was nothing distinctive about its aroma. It was still pleasing to inhale, like all perfumes that flowers produced were. Miel had no clue what it was going to taste like based on this interesting scent, and so he took the plunge and bit into the large flower head.

"Ah! That is...is that what spicy tastes like?" Miel asked,

caught by surprise by the somewhat... hot sensation that was settling on his tongue. It was neither 'sweet' or 'bitter,' but seemed to have a flavour that was completely different to that. "Is it spicy?"

"Almost, it is peppery. But it is a fascinating flavour, mmm?" Satariel replied, enthusiastically chewing his own chrysanthemum. "Do you like it, little angel?"

"My tongue feels warm." Miel placed the flower stem down on his thigh and reached up to touch at his lips. The peppery taste was making his tongue and lips tingle slightly, which was a sensation that he greatly enjoyed. "I like it a lot!"

The final flower that Satariel had selected for them to taste was one that had many small blooms on it, as opposed to a single head. The flowers had small, white petals in bunches of five, with bright, yellow centres. Though they were very simple to look at, he thought they were very beautiful.

After some study and sniffing, Miel realised it was angelica, with its musky and heady aroma. He took a bite to find that its taste was something else. "What is this taste, Satariel?" he asked in wonder, letting the somewhat woody and unusual flavour soak into his tongue.

Was it tart or sweet? Miel couldn not tell, but the flavour was impossible to describe.

"How do you describe it?"

"Angelica tastes like liquorice to me, little angel," Satariel explained, though this was something that Miel had no knowledge of in regards to taste. "Aniseed sometimes – it is a strange taste, is it not?"

"Hmm, I think I like that flavour the most," Miel hummed, before lifting the flower to his mouth to take another bite.

"Little angel?" Satariel suddenly said, holding his own flower in front of his face to study the small flower heads, rather than eat it.

"Yes, my dearest dæmon?" Miel replied with a soft smile, and he cheeked the petals so he could savour the flavour for a moment before swallowing it.

"I have been feeling the strangest feelings inside of me these last few days; emotions that I would dare not voice aloud.

Yet I feel that I must voice to you," Satariel said in a quiet voice. He stared into the tightly bloomed petals as if he was divining the future in its stigma and stamens. "I feel like... like I can tell you about my own doubts and worries because you have such an intelligent and beautiful rumination on life."

Miel slowly lowered the angelica flower from his face at this, giving the dæmon his full attention and watching him playing with his own flower as he tried to think of what he wanted to say.

"Being in your company, however short that might be, has made me want to... to do things. Small acts that seem to be rooted in kindness, or goodness. Things that I should not think of doing, and yet I cannot ignore even when I want to."

Satariel glanced up from the flower to look up at him for a moment, holding his gaze as he asked, "Do you think that is strange?"

"Why should I find such a thing strange, Satariel? I think that... that you and I are already so alike," Miel replied, and he placed the flower down in his lap so he could reach over and take hold of his wrist. "You feel such powerful emotions like guilt already, even when I thought that dæmons could not feel such emotions for their actions. To me, this means you are capable of committing such acts of kindness too. So, why do you think it strange?"

"Because I have never done such acts before!" Satariel cried out in exasperation. He turned his face away from him because he could not seem to hold his gaze. "How can you know that I would be able to commit such acts of kindness, if I have never shown any kindness to anything?!"

"You spared that butterfly earlier, until we discovered her broken wing," Miel stated, as he entwined their fingers together. "You could have swallowed her whole, but you stopped when I begged you to not eat her. That was an act of mercy, even if it was misguided."

"Did I spare her, Miel? Or did I simply stop in surprise?" he asked in reply, his expression showing that he was confused and woeful.

"What do you believe in your heart, Satariel?"

Satariel fell silent at this as he thought his question over intently. Miel could see his black eyes glinting in the current dawn sunlight, even when he had his head held low to avoid his gaze. It was apparent that he was consciously searching his mind for the true answer. After a moment, he broke his silence.

"I... I think that I stopped eating the butterfly because you surprised me. But I think that I could... could spare one from being eaten too, if I wanted to," Satariel said in a soft voice, as he reached up to give his horn a series of strokes. "I have never tried to spare something before, but I really do think that I could. Do... do you, little angel?"

"I know that you could, Satariel; and do you know how I know this?"

"Mmm?" Satariel hummed, as he glanced over at him and paused in the act of playing with his horn.

"Satariel, you were picking flowers for me, and there were butterflies *all* around you!" Miel declared, throwing his arms out for emphasis and drawing his attention to the dozens of insects that were still lingering in the flower patch. "You did not even look at them because you were so busy finding flowers for us to eat. To me, that means you spared those butterflies without even thinking about it."

Satariel slowly turned his head to look at the flowers, and it was only then that he seemed to realise they were surrounded by butterflies. The surprise was enough to make him drop his hand down to his lap, his breath leaving his slack lips in a soft sigh. He tracked a white cabbage butterfly all the way up into the sky before losing sight of it, and then he turned back to him with a dazed smile.

"Satariel, there was a moment when you were hunkered down right next to a particularly lazy butterfly. You could have easily snatched it up and ate it, but you did not," Miel continued, as he reached over to take hold of his shoulders and gave them a soft squeeze. "To me, that is an act of total mercy, and one that you should be proud of."

"I... I *am* proud, Miel," Satariel agreed with a nod. "I saw those butterflies, but I did not want to eat them because I was busy with the flowers. I *could have* eaten them, but I... I did not."

Miel gave Satariel a proud smile, and he was able to sense just how happy that the dæmon was to have managed such a small act of mercy and kindness.

If he could manage this, then there really was a high chance that Satariel could manage other small acts too. Perhaps nothing too grand, like singing hallowed praises to God. Maybe something simple and kind, like caretaker duties.

"Come, let us go back to the glen," Miel suggested, cocking his head in the direction of the trees. "I need to tend to the shrine today. Would you like to assist me, Satariel?"

Satariel took a moment to think this request over, rather than reply right away. Miel could see the hesitation in his rounded eyes, mixed in with trepidation and a burst of something that might just have been courage. Then he gave him a soft nod in agreement, silently telling him that he would be his assistant.

Before leaving the flower patch, Satariel was sure to gather another ample bouquet of flowers that he could nibble on.

Miel watched him selecting his choices, noting that he completely ignored the butterflies once more as he did so. Amidst the vibrant orange, pink, and purple blooms, he had selected quite the number of fluffy, white angelica flowers. When they entered the copse of trees, he held one of them out to him in offering.

Walking through the woods again, carefully stepping over the treacherous roots and vines, Miel found that the journey was even more enjoyable now that he had the sweet and addictive taste of angelica flowers on his tongue. He still could not seem to figure out the exact way to describe the taste, but he knew that he loved it.

Satariel could enjoy his sweet and spicy flowers, and he would savour the liquorice ones.

Upon reaching the felled trunk, Miel did not carelessly pick up Satariel, for fear that he really had not enjoyed his earlier introduction to flying. He lingered back for a moment to see what he would do, assuming that the dæmon would clamber over the trunk like he had been planning to do so before. But when he turned to look back over his shoulder at him, he realised that Satariel actually wanted to take to the sky again.

"Are you sure, Satariel?" Miel asked, as he moved to stand behind him and placed his hands on his waist. "You might get dizzy again."

"The first time that you did it, you did not tell me," Satariel replied, taking hold of his wrists so he could gently take his hands off his waist and wrap his arms around him more securely. "You frightened me; that is why I got so dizzy. What do you do before flying, little angel?"

"Take a deep breath, I find that that helps," he suggested, settling his chin down on the dæmon's shoulder and looking down to see that he was holding onto his forearms. "Try to not look down too, not at first. That will scare you even more. Maybe you could close your eyes, if that is what scares you? Are you ready, my dearest dæmon?"

"I am ready, little angel," Satariel confirmed, closing his eyes and tightening his hold on his arms. "Take me to the sky."

Miel beat his wings softly a few times because he wanted to slowly build up momentum and then lift off from the ground, rather than shoot right up like he had done so before.

When they left the ground again, Satariel instinctively tensed up in his hold, his pent-up breath leaving him in a soft grunt. But Miel could sense that he was less frightened this time.

Rather than soar over the trunk and drop back down in the grass on the other side, Miel stayed in the air for a moment longer.

"See? It is not so frightening; is it, Satariel?" he remarked, as they hovered just several feet above the ground. "I am not going to let go, you are safe in my arms."

Satariel slowly opened his eyes, his lips pulled into a thin line because he was clearly still a little scared. Miel heard him gulping as he looked down at the ground.

With every quick beat of Miel's wings to keep them in place, the grass beneath their bare feet almost danced; blown this way and that by the gusts of air. The tree leaves rustled up a storm, shaking and whispering like hushed voices in the quiet woods.

"No," Satariel replied in a quiet voice. "No, it is not frightening, little angel. It… it actually feels nice."

As he gently lowered them to the ground, Miel saw the way that Satariel's expression turned slack with wonder instead of fear. His filthy toes twitched from the ticklish blades of grass touching his skin, which made him let out a breathy sound much like a laugh.

This time, Satariel was steady on his feet when they landed, somewhat bouncy and not weak and shaking. Miel knew that he was going to want to try flying more and more now, and he could already foresee the dæmon requesting he take him to the sky many more times.

After overcoming the tree trunk, they only had to walk along the thick and wild path to get back to the glen. When they broke through the trees and stepped back into the little clearing, Miel's ears were once more blessed with the sound of songbirds and chirping insects, and he crossed the glen to stop in front of the cave.

Satariel positively dragged his feet over to him, playing with the gnawed remains of his bouquet and staring down at their feet to avoid looking at the dark mouth of the grotto.

"Do you want to hold my hand, my dearest dæmon?" Miel offered, holding it out to him and lightly tinkling his fingers. "I can understand your fear. This is a momentous thing for you to do, and I think that you are a very brave dæmon. In fact, I think you are the bravest dæmon and–"

Before he could finish this bold statement, Satariel dropped his flower stems and moved to take hold of his hand. His grip was tight, alluding to his anxious state, and so Miel took hold and strengthened the hold by slotting his fingers between his.

When Miel stepped inside of the cave, he almost had to drag Satariel in behind him. The dæmon was not digging his heels into the ground exactly, but he was still hesitant enough to give a little resistance. But upon his arm entering the shadowy mouth of the cave and nothing happening to him, he allowed him to gently tug him inside.

As expected, Satariel did not burst into flames or start shrieking in tongues, nor did he even wince with a slight hint of pain or discomfort. No, he slowly lowered his hunched shoulders with a soft sigh and stared at the alabaster statue of the holy mother and child with his round and curious eyes.

"See, it is nothing to be frightened of," Miel said with a soft smile. "It might seem frightening at first, but the shrine is mortal-made. It contains spiritual energy, but it is not intrinsically holy ground. This cave is no more holy than the flower patch, or the stream. It is devotion and praise that makes it so."

"Does that mean Heaven is only holy because of devotion and praise?" Satariel asked suddenly, as he turned away from the statue to look at him.

"It may just be so, my dearest dæmon," Miel replied with a gentle shrug, his wings ruffling from the movement. "It might just be that holiness exists only when personal devotion exists. Being the way that God made me, I am incapable of existing without devotion, and so, I cannot see the world in any other way. But you can, Satariel, and so you must understand holiness much clearer than I can."

"I do not know about holiness exactly, but I know you are the most perfect being that I have been blessed to encounter," Satariel said, as he took several steps closer to the shrine and reached out to tentatively touch it with his fingertips. He darted them over the surface of the base of the statue, which was spotless and free from even a hint of dust. "Therefore, I believe every single thing that you say."

"Oh, Satariel," Miel almost gushed, as he reached up to cover his smile with his fingers. "You should not believe me, just like that. Even if I am blessed to be so enlightened. I am made in God's image, but only God is truly perfect and blessed with total knowledge."

"I am incapable of believing in God, but I am not incapable of believing in you, little angel," Satariel replied, as his fingertips roamed across the smooth, alabaster expanse of the holy mother's naked foot – which was peeping free from the folds of her flowing mantel.

For some reason, Satariel's words struck a chord deep down inside of him that made Miel's chest and cheeks flood with warmth. It diffused through his body down to his very fingers and toes, and he wished he knew *why* he felt such a sensation... because he was currently unable to ascertain the reason.

"Besides, if you are made in God's image... you must be as perfect as God is," Satariel finished, as he dropped his hand back down to his side and resumed running his eyes across the shrine instead. "I hope that I do not offend you by saying such things. But before meeting an angel, I had thought them monstrous and terrifying beings. Now, because of you, I know them to be beautiful and tender."

"I had thought the same about dæmons too. But thanks to you, I now know otherwise," Miel agreed, moving to stand beside him. "Dæmons are actually intelligent, thoughtful, and fascinating beings."

There were several candles placed on the shrine base, which had melted out across the alabaster from use and age. Miel conjured up a spark of fire with a quick click of his fingers, setting the aged wicks alight and making Satariel jump in surprise.

Clearly, the dæmon had not known that he could do such small acts of creation, and so he stared at the flickering flames in wonder.

"An act of kindness can be a simple act," Miel explained, as he retrieved a broom from the corner of the grotto and held it out to him. "It need not be something grand or meticulously planned. Kindness is as simple as helping a beetle get back onto its legs when it cannot do so itself. Kindness is burying seeds back into the ground in the hopes of growing a tree. It can even be something just like this – sweeping dirt out of the shrine."

Satariel accepted the broom from him and got the light chunk of oak into both hands to heft its weight. The bristles were made of tough and dried sorghum leaves, and they did a great job of cleaning up the debris that blew inside the cave. The dæmon eyed the broom for several seconds, and then he slowly lowered it to the ground and started attempting to sweep.

At first, his actions were fumbling and uncertain, for he kept shaking the broom back and forth like a pendulum to sweep the leaves around his feet. But he slowly started to figure out the right way of sweeping with some practise.

Miel retrieved his hardy reed bucket and brush from the back of the cave, and he filled it with water from the stream just through the copse of trees. When he returned, he saw Satariel was smiling as he softly swept the broom to the side. He had yet to figure out that he could *gather* the leaves together into a pile and then sweep them outside, and so he was just brushing little clumps of strays leaves out at a time.

Miel stayed in the mouth of the cave for a few seconds to observe him, seeing the warm and soft candlelight playing off his smiling face and glinting in his eyes. Such a mischievous, little dæmon he might just be, but there was something good inside of him too – something redeemable and passionate that Miel knew was worth aiding.

Satariel noticed that he was watching him after a moment, and so he glanced up as he swept a mixture of leaves, dried-up flowers petals, and tiny rodent bones out into the grass. Then he gave him a content smile that showed he was pleased with himself, his dark eyes crinkling at the corners so beautifully.

Miel returned the smile before crossing the cave again and placing the heavy bucket down by his feet. He dunked the horse hair brush into the chill water, and then he lowered himself to his knees to begin softly scrubbing at the bottom of the statue.

The statue was free from any hints of dust or dirt, but he washed it more as a purification process than to truly cleanse it. The water was clear and pure, and washing the holy mother and child with it was his way of showing his devotion.

"Even when this act is so small, you feel much better for doing it; do you not?" Miel asked, glancing up as he scrubbed at the shrine base to watch him sweeping up the leaves.

"I do," Satariel agreed, brushing another pile of debris out of the cave. "It is just like when we bathed our feet in the stream and we washed away all of the dirt. I feel that brushing away this dirt will leave me feeling... clean too."

Miel felt his hand slipping off the base of the statue, the brush having shifted too close to the edge so that he shifted from the sudden change in momentum. As he dropped the brush in surprise, he felt his palm brushing against the base, and then something almost... catching in his skin. It felt like a streak of heat coursing along his hand, a sensation that he had never felt before.

For a few seconds, Miel could do nothing more than stare at his stinging palm in complete shock. But then the shocking sight of blood beading up in the scratch, welling so much that it started spilling free to run down his wrist, was enough to make his breath leave his lungs in a wheeze of horror.

Miel had just sliced his hand open on the chipped and sharp corner of the statue base.

"Huh? *Blood?*"

Across the cave, Satariel froze up at his cry of horror. The broomstick slipped out of his grip to land at his feet with a soft thumping sound, a puff of dust taking to the air. Then he darted over to him and dropped to his knees to snatch hold of his hand and forearm and drag them close to look at the injury.

"The... the statue," Miel stuttered, as a fat bead of blood spilled free and ran over the curve of his thumb to drop down onto his bare knee. "I slipped and my hand... blood, I–"

Satariel moved so fast that Miel had no clue what he was doing until he felt the hot and wet sensation of his tongue lapping at his skin.

Satariel had just *licked* at his blood.

Instinctively, Miel pulled his hand out of his grip and brought it close to his chest, his eyes wide with complete shock.

Satariel flinched at the sudden movement, blinking rapidly and closing his fingers around thin air. He dragged his gaze up from his injured hand to look at him, and Miel saw the horror slowly dawning on his features when he realised what he had just done.

"I am sorry," he managed to say, his lips still smeared with his blood and his tongue desperately slipping out to lap at it. "I am sorry, I did not mean to, I just– the sight of it, the scent of it, I could not stop myself! Oh!"

Satariel threw himself at him, collapsing onto his lap and lying prostrate across his thighs in a limp manner. His little horns were digging into the curve of his stomach, not tight enough to tear his tunic and sink into his skin, but enough to lightly dimple it.

"Oh, Miel, I am sorry," Satariel moaned in a heavily muffled voice, his feet writhing around in the dirt as he twisted and turned in something like anguish. *"Please, forgive me, I did not mean to! It was like the butterfly all over again – some disgusting compulsion that I could not seem to control!"*

"It is alright, Satariel," Miel said, as he lowered his hand from his chest and reached down to give him a soft shoulder pat. "It surprised me, was all. I did not think that you would… would do that. But you do not need to apologise to me. Please, Satariel, sit up and look at me."

Miel had to nudge at his shoulder with his uninjured hand several times, encouraging Satariel to sit upright again. The dæmon kept his head held low, and he could see that tears were running down his cheeks freely, gathering on his jawline before dripping down into their laps. His tunic skirt was damp from his tears, wet patches spreading out across the pink silk.

The sight of his tears made Miel cup his chin in his hand, angling his face so he could look at him. "Why are you crying, Satariel?" he asked in a soothing voice. "What is the matter?"

"I-I did something good, and then I ruined it," Satariel moaned, rubbing his bunched-up fists against his streaming eyes. "I wuh-was trying to show you how guh-good that I could be, but I cannot ever do something good without-out doing something cruel!"

"Satariel, you did not do anything bad," Miel disagreed with a firm head shake. "It might have been… misguided, perhaps, but it was not bad. Cruelty and bad actions require intent, and you just made a mistake, is all. You did not hurt me, just surprised me. It did not negate the goodness that you showed me by brushing up all that dirt, I promise you."

"It duh-did not?" Satariel hiccuped, dropping his hands and blinking tears away to try and hold his gaze.

"Not at all," Miel reaffirmed, as he wiped at his damp cheek for him with his thumb. "Here."

When he held his hand out to him once more, Satariel glanced between his bloody palm and face rapidly, confused by what he was offering.

"It is alright, I trust you, Satariel," Miel said with a warm smile. "There is nothing wrong or sinful about... about licking my blood. It is no more sinful than me eating those flowers. If you had have hurt me first, it would have been cruel, but–"

"I could never," Satariel gasped, as he took hold of his hand again to entwine their fingers together. "How could I hurt an angel, and not just any angel, but such a little angel?"

Miel laughed softly at this, letting the dæmon bring his hand up to his face so he could sniff at the blood that was still slowly trickling free from the slice in his palm.

"But you did not hurt me, Satariel, and so there is nothing to be upset or apologetic for," Miel finished with a smile. "I would just end up washing it free with water, so, what difference does it make, hmm?"

Despite giving him permission, Satariel hesitated before parting his lips again and lapping his tongue out. Just like before, it felt hot and wet against Miel's skin because the dæmon must have absorbed a lot of his radiance this dawn. The sensation was ticklish, made his fingers lightly curl up against his palm and his breath escape him in a soft sigh.

Satariel trailed his tongue over the heel of his hand as gentle as could be, his eyelids fluttering closed as he curled his tongue back into his mouth and swallowed the mixture of blood and saliva. He must have savoured the flavour, judging from his serene expression, but Miel would not know. He had never tasted blood before, and he certainly did not want to – not even his own blood.

Satariel nuzzled his lips and nose in the dip of his palm, chasing after the slightest smears of blood until his skin was clean once more.

"I have never cut my skin before," Miel confided in a quiet voice, letting Satariel tenderly rub his thumb across his injured palm. "Not once, in all of my existence. That must be rather strange to you, Satariel, but it is true."

"Why do you assume I have cut my own flesh?" Satariel asked, slowly rolling his eyes up to look at him.

Miel stared at him for a moment, taken by surprise by his question. There was something almost defensive on the dæmon's face, as if he had said something that had touched a nerve. He quickly explained, "Your feet are covered in scars, you told me that you have cut them many times on rocks and such. So, you must know what it feels like to have your skin scratch, tear, and bleed. I... I once heard that dæmons hurt themselves for pleasure, but I do not think that you do that, Satariel. Do dæmons do that?"

"Flagellation is still rather common in my kind," Satariel replied, as he resumed stroking his thumb over his now clean palm. "I will bet that the angels do not whip themselves, but you can bet that dæmons do."

"Satariel, are the scars on your feet from rocks, or did you used to... to whip yourself like that too?" Miel asked him in a whisper-soft voice. "I only ask because, well, you have shown so much remorse and pain over these several days, and I was worried that you might just have done such a thing."

"... I did, a long time ago," he replied in a quiet voice. "It is a practice I no longer do, but I used to. But not for pleasure, little angel, not at all."

"You felt guilty, did you not?" Miel asked, his voice a low whisper as he lifted his gaze up to look at Satariel's face. "You did it to hurt yourself because you thought that you deserved to suffer. But you do not, Satariel, you do not deserve to suffer."

"I never would have thought that possible before meeting you, little angel," Satariel said, as he took hold of his hand to cradle it between the both of his and entwined their fingers together. "I am still trying to accept the thought that... that I exist with purpose and meaning; that I am not cruel or evil, but that there is some... design in me that made me this way – just like you told me. But now... now, I am not so sure I should suffer like that."

"What did the pain bring you, Satariel? Did it bring you any clarity? An understanding to your existence, or relief from your mental and spiritual torment?"

"No, just more pain."

"Then there is no reason to suffer; is there?" Miel moved so he could sit beside him and place his head down on his shoulder. "Suffering is evil, Satariel. It is something that I am yet to understand, though I know in time that I might just find answers, if I search deeply enough. No being should suffer, not even dæmons. All that it brought you was pain and scars – it was meaningless suffering."

At this, they fell silent. The only noise that entered the cave was the soft sound of songbirds tweeting, and the distant babbling of the brook water.

Miel reached over with his free hand to find Satariel's foot, and he clasped it in his hold so he could once more feel those patches of scarred tissue against his fingertips.

"Little angel?"

"Yes, Satariel?" he replied, angling his face to look up at him.

"Are you going to sing praise again?" Satariel asked, as he gently placed his cheek against the top of his head. "I liked listening to you singing yesterday."

"Of course, I always sing praise during my duties, and there is still work to be done," Miel explained, his gaze shifting to look over at the bucket of water and brush just a few feet away. "Do dæmons sing, hmm?"

"No, not like the way that you sing, little angel. I think that might be why I liked listening to it so much. But it might also be because your voice made me feel like I was being... cleansed – blessed, even."

Miel moved to gently knock his head away, twisting to look at the dæmon because he could feel an idea growing in his mind. "You should sing with me."

"Ah, I cannot sing, Miel, I would ruin your beautiful praises with my voice, and-"

"Satariel, singing is something that all beings can do: little creatures, mortals, and little dæmons too," Miel said with a mischievous smile. "You just have to try it, that is all."

"Just try it?" Satariel repeated, twitching his brow and sticking his tongue out to wet his lips. "Are you sure?"

"All music is beautiful music, my dearest dæmon. Be it mortal instruments and voices, the songs of birds and bugs and all the little creatures – it is all beautiful. I will start, hmm, and then you can join in whenever you wish."

Miel took several deep breaths to ready himself for singing praise, feeling his chest expanding with every single inhale so he would be able to reach pure and powerful notes with ease. He could see Satariel was so frightfully nervous at the thought of singing with him.

But when Miel opened his lips and let the first string of notes bleed out into the still cave air, the dæmon's entire demeanour changed. His tense muscles relaxed as he let his own breath out in a soft sigh, his eyelids closing and his lips turning slack.

No words ever came out of Miel's lips when he sang praise, for no words could ever be fitting to utter to God. They contained no power, no meaning or form, and therefore only rich notes could only be suitable for praise. Sometimes, words might unknowingly spill free when he was deeply immersed in his worship, but Miel paid them no mind.

How strange it must be for Satariel to hear these notes leaving his lips – without substance or meaning, but carrying emotion far greater than words ever could.

Did he find it strange?

Did he search his mind for a language that fitted these utterances? Or did he understand in a way that completely transcended these boundaries?

Miel did not know, but he did see the way that Satariel completely dived down deep into his praises. He looked almost hypnotised by his voice, his body falling still save for his soft breathing.

96

When Satariel started singing, he did not try and replicate his aria like he had assumed, rather he accompanied his voice by way of deeply humming. At first, he did so so quietly that he could hardly hear him. But he started to increase his volume as he grew more confident, and Miel was finally able to hear his voice.

Oh, dæmons might not sing, but Satariel's voice was like nothing he had ever imagined. It was deep, much like his speaking voice, but it was not monotonous in any way. It was a pleasingly mellow timbre, which flattered his own moderate and oftentimes high pitch in the most wonderful of ways.

Before he could help himself, Miel leapt to his feet, and he dragged Satariel up with him. He started to move around as he sang, spinning and taking large steps round and round that were almost like a dance.

Satariel tried so hard to sing with him, but he struggled to suppress his urge to laugh. His hums turned into wheezy chuckles, before turning into full-blown laughter as he threw his head back and let him spin him in dizzying circles until the pair of them ended up dropping to their knees.

Miel burst out into ecstatic giggles, his head spinning and his legs too weak to possibly stand on. He could not seem to control himself and neither could Satariel, for the dæmon sank back against the earth and pulled him down with him. Their chests connected and luckily they did not clash heads with one another, as that certainly would not have helped their dizziness.

"Oh, Satariel, I must go back and continue tending to the pastures. But will you return here this dusk? I *must* see you again, I must," Miel begged, taking hold of his hand and placing it down on his ribs to feel his racing heartbeat through his thin chest.

"Little angel, I will be here when you return," he promised, as he squeezed his hand tightly within his own. "I will come running, if I must."

"Can we carry on tasting things, my dearest dæmon? Ah, I long to taste even more things, and–"

Satariel spoke over him, "Miel, we can do whatever you

desire. Taste whatever you want, sing whatever you want – anything you wish."

"Satariel, does this make us… friends?" Miel asked, and he felt an eddy of nervousness spreading into his belly as he looked down at his face.

"I have never had a friend before," Satariel confessed in a whisper.

"Me neither. Are we… I mean, do you want to be my friend, Satariel?"

"I cannot think of a better friend than you," he replied with a lazy grin. "My precious, little angel."

"Oh!" Miel gushed, his wings pulling in close and then spreading wide open again as his lips lifted in a happy smile. "That made me feel so… so good, Satariel – so good! Is this what friendship is supposed to feel like?"

"I think it is what happiness feels like," Satariel remarked, as he reached up to brush a lock of his hair back behind his ear and returned the smile.

IV

The sight of the darkening evening sky below his feet was something that Miel had been anticipating for what seemed like an eternity now. Being out in the pastures, he was able to gaze down onto the mortal plane from his dizzying height and watch the very rotations of the clouds and constellations. He loved to do so whilst he was singing praise, or when he was meditating.

Currently, Miel could see the sun was starting to set on his favourite spot on the whole of the plane – his little woody sanctuary. The fading sunlight was throwing burnt orange and pink rays all across the sky. This was a sign that evening was steadfastly approaching, and soon enough it would be dusk.

Sitting on his favoured cliff top ledge of choice, his legs dangling over the precipice and lightly kicking back and forth in rhythm with his soft singing, Miel had been delivering constant praise whilst working on something special for most of the day.

Something special *and* secret, which was a gift for his new dæmon friend. Said gift was currently stored within his tunic, just waiting to be given to him the very moment that they saw each other again.

Miel studied the sky below his feet for a moment, and then he moved to stand upright. He had to delicately brush hints of dust free from his bare thighs and the lengths of his tunic; he was doing so in an attempt at neatening up his appearance because he had taken the time to carefully brush and preen his wing feathers today. He had done so between his duties, of course, as he had had quite a lot to do.

Miel had tended to the pastures with his fellow brothers and sisters, sowing seeds and flooding the grass with blessed water to sustain the souls that it nurtured. He had helped cleanse the lambs by way of nursing and cradling them in his arms, to help them let go of their previous lives and sins so they could become untainted and be reborn into another mortal vessel and continue their undying life cycle. He had sung praise without end, just to ensure he had contributed enough devotion to please God and allow him to go back to the mortal plane to see Satariel. And now, it was finally time to go down to the woods to see his friend once more.

But before he went down Heaven's bridge to do so, there was just one more thing that he wanted to do.

Miel turned on his heel to go back into the pasture, walking towards his current flock that consisted of a hundred lambs he was entrusted to bless and teach. They were currently grazing in the lush grass all around him. But at his beckoning, they all stopped and proceeding to toddle over to him – bleating and jumping around his legs.

"God is good, sweet lambs, God is good!" Miel gushed, reaching down to lift up one of the lambs to hug it tight against his chest. He lowered himself down into the grass so he could mingle with them for a moment. "I tell you this every dawn, but I must tell you once more!"

As Miel settled down on his knees, the other lambs flocked around him, vying for attention. Such beautiful souls they were – with their honeyed eyes that were thickly lashed with white, their soft, pink noses and lips, and their fuzzy ears that he so loved to rub between his fingers and thumbs.

Miel had to move the lamb into the crook of his arm to reach out with his free hand and stroke at the others. The sensation of their warm, cotton-soft wool made him giggle, as it felt so luxurious against his skin.

"God rewarded my piety with a friend! My own special friend!" he declared, unable to control the urge to grin at them. "My friend has taught me so much, he has opened my eyes to many things that I had never thought to think about before. He calls me 'an enlightened being,' but I feel at my most enlightened when we spend time together."

The lambs were all staring up at him, so innocent and agog at his words, that he knew they would sit with him all evening long and listen.

Before meeting Satariel, he had spent great deals of time feeding his flock sweet flowers and just sharing with them his musings on existence and divinity. As a result, he knew just how loving the souls could be.

"Ah, it may be so that I once thought his kind were soulless beings, but I am beginning to see the truth," Miel said with a soft sigh, as another adventurous lamb climbed up onto his free thigh and gently head-butted at his upper arm. "All beings, even the little creatures, possess souls. Little creatures are without sin, and so their souls are reborn instantly into new vessels – unlike mortals like you. But dæmons? Dæmons are so full of sin that they can never *be* reborn, and so their souls live on for an eternity, just like angel souls! It makes so much sense, sweet lambs! How did I never realise this before?!"

The lambs let out a mixture of bleats at this; possibly agreeing with him, or possibly wondering if he had any more flowers tucked away inside of his tunic to feed to them.

"But even a sinner can seek redemption and forgiveness," he remarked, giving the adventurous lamb a quick head stroke. "Just like what Satariel seems to be doing. Maybe, he cannot be without sin, but that does not mean that he is evil. He sins because God made him that way, that is what I think, sweet lambs."

Miel moved to place the two lambs back down in the grass and get to his feet. He brushed his hands against his tunic skirt as he looked down at them, giving them all a warm and loving smile.

"Now, I am going to visit my dæmon friend and learn more fascinating things from him. Be sure to slumber in my absence because slumber will help you all heal. I will return to care for you at dawn, sweet lambs."

Heaven's bridge ran all the way around the kingdom. It was the gateway that his kind used to go down to the mortal plane, and which souls used to ascend to Heaven after passing. It appeared to be nothing more than a veil, a golden shimmer of light that poured down from the pastures like a waterfall. But it was as solid as the earth itself.

Miel almost skipped down Heaven's bridge because he was so giddy, his feet softly padding on the veil to make it shimmer musically beneath him. He could feel something almost pulsing away in his chest that just had to be excitement. It made him feel breathless, and it flooded his body with a great warmth.

Down beneath him, the mortal plane resumed spinning, and the skies started to grow purple in parts as the sun started to set on the horizon. Miel might just make it down there whilst the sky was still pink, and so he beat his wings hard to propel himself down the bridge as fast as he could fly.

Was Satariel this excited to see him again – his angelic friend? Was he racing along the woody path and clambering over tree trunks in his haste to reach the clearing to wait for him to arrive? Miel could only hope that it was so.

Upon touching down on the earthen plane with a springy bounce, Miel carried on skipping through the grassy field that would take him into the woods. His wings were just begging to be used, trembling in anticipation, but the woods were far too thick to fly through. If he were the size of a songbird, perhaps he could soar between the trees and flit his way down into the clearing with ease. But he was far too large for that – even if he was a 'little angel.'

Miel had never walked through the woods so quickly before, and his eagerness meant he did not even pause to try and observe any little creatures that might be hidden away in the underbrush like usual. He just raced along the natural path as quickly as he could, eager to reunite with his dæmon friend so they could spend the entire dusk together.

"Oh, Satariel!" Miel called, as he stepped into the clearing. He cupped his hands around his mouth to amplify his voice. "Where are you, my dearest dæmon?!"

Miel lowered his hands to his chest, playing with the neckline of his silken tunic. After just a mere moment of waiting, the sound of something rustling echoed throughout the clearing, and it grew louder and louder as something approached.

When Miel turned his head to track the sound, he could see bushes rattling hard all around the pussy willow, and then his dæmonic friend burst free from them.

"Little angel!" Satariel exclaimed, as he ducked underneath the tree branches and raced into the glen. There was a noticeable skip in his step that brought a smile to Miel's lips, for he looked so happy this dusk. "Little angel! I brought you something, I brought you something, and–"

Satariel's toes caught on a tree root, and so he stumbled forward, but Miel managed to catch him just in time to save him from a nasty fall.

"Careful, my dearest dæmon!" Miel declared, tugging him upright and giving him a warm and welcoming smile. "You must watch where you are going, you cannot fly like I can. But you almost did just then!"

Satariel chuckled at this, as he reached up to rub at one of his horns. There was a high colour to his cheeks that looked to be pure excitement, and even when his skin was currently chill, Miel just knew it would be warm again soon enough.

Such flushed cheeks! Such a wide smile that revealed to him his many pointy, little teeth!

Yes, Satariel *was* as excited as he was to see him again, and the knowledge that the dæmon was so happy was enough to make his knees feel weak.

"What did you bring, hmm, Satariel?" Miel asked, as he let go of his arms and dropped his gaze to look at the curious sight of a belt now present on his body.

There were a variety of small glass jars dangling from a leather thong that Satariel had knotted around his svelte waist, and they tinkled loudly when they bumped together. Miel studied them with a great fascination to see they were storing liquid of some kind, but he could not clearly see what it was because of the dim lighting in the clearing.

Satariel eyed the jars before selecting one and pulling it free from the loop of twine attached to his belt. It had a thick cork stopper shoved inside it to keep the liquid trapped within, but it was otherwise undecorated.

"Honey!" Satariel declared, as he lifted up the glass jar and tipped it. The viscous fluid slowly spread over the glass side, catching the dim sunlight to glow a vivid, amber colour. "Several different kinds! I gathered it this morning from *all* across the woods and from the village at the bottom of the mountain – just for you!"

"You did?" Miel asked in surprise, glancing down at the

four glass jars dangling from his belt to see a rainbow variety of honey clashing against his rough, black tunic. "Satariel, that must have taken you such a long time!"

"I had nothing to do whilst you were tending to the pastures," Satariel explained with a soft shrug. "Gathering honeycomb from hives is hard work, and I do not want you getting stung. I decided to collect you some, so you could taste it too. You have tasted the flowers, and I thought that you would love sampling honey this evening."

"Thank you, Satariel, that is so sweet of you."

Miel really was thankful that his dæmon friend had went to such great lengths just for him. A single sample of honey would have been wonderful, and yet Satariel had collected five different samples, just so that he could learn to taste them all and find his favourite one.

That was sweeter than honey itself – supposing that honey was indeed sweet, like Miel had always assumed.

Satariel shifted to sit down in the grass, patting at the ground in silent invitation for him to join him.

Miel lowered himself to his knees, sitting on his heels and folding his hands in his lap primly. He was eager to sample the honey, just like he had been with the flowers, because he knew that mortals greatly loved this nectar for some reason. The fact that Satariel also savoured it meant he longed to understand the complexities of honey too.

"The first one that we should try is wildflower honey..."

Satariel carefully popped the cork stopper free from the jar before holding it out to him. The scent wafted from the glass, and so he leaned closer to take a deep inhale of it.

Miel breathed in the scent, his lips lifting up into a natural smile because the perfume was so pleasing to his nose. He knew that scents could be deceiving thanks to the flowers, and so he did not know what to expect at all. But he was more than ready to sample every single one of the different honeys.

"When you taste honey, let it settle on your tongue and then slowly swallow it," Satariel instructed, miming that he should scoop honey out of the jar with his finger. "That way, you can taste *and* smell the honey for a moment."

Miel coated his forefinger with the amber honey, and he was shocked by just how thick and sticky that it was on his skin. Then he slipped his finger into his mouth. As he sucked the honey free, he let it settle on his tongue to overwhelm his senses with a sugary sweetness that was far more powerful than the carnations had been.

"Oh, Satariel! My tongue has flooded with saliva just from the small swallow – it is *that* sweet!" he declared, before swallowing the mixture of honey and saliva.

Satariel sucked a dribble of honey off his own finger and ran his tongue around his mouth, and then he made a series of pleased noises under his breath. "Wildflower honey is hard to predict," he explained around the sample. "No matter how much I sniffed at it whilst bleeding the honeycomb, I could not ascertain the full flavour alone. It seems to be a blend of so many flowers. But it was very sweet, just like I was hoping it would be. Would you like some more?"

"I want to taste them all first!" Miel said enthusiastically, and so his dæmon friend let out a laugh and shoved the cork stopper back into the jar. "I must find my favourite one!"

The next jar that Satariel selected was also a rich, golden shade, with a hint of reddish-orange trapped within the thick liquid. When he popped the chunk of cork free, the scent that wafted from the jar was unexpectedly fruity – a citrus blend that instantly made Miel think of bright colours, like yellows and oranges.

Miel gathered some of the honey onto his finger and licked it free, and he discovered it was as fruity as it had smelled – if not more so. He did not know if he liked the citrusy honey more or less than the sugary wildflower sweetness, but he knew that he enjoyed both of them immensely.

Judging from the way that Satariel eagerly sucked up a thick dribble of the red-tinged honey, he liked this variety a lot too.

"Orange blossom honey is a good example of fruity honey," Satariel explained, as he sealed the jar again to secure it onto his belt. "It is also a very rich shade, so it is pretty to look at."

"I think it is lovely," Miel agreed after swallowing the mouthful. "It has that hint of citrus to it that matches its scent and colour – it is not misleading like the flowers were."

This made Satariel snort laughter as he retrieved the third glass jar, which contained a runny and deep brown honey, rather than thick and golden. Unlike the previous two honeys, it had a somewhat earthen scent that made Miel furrow his brow slightly as he breathed it in.

Ah, this was a scent that could mean many things – spicy, mild, maybe even herbal. He was going to have to taste it to find out.

"Oh, this one tastes faintly... like lemons," Miel said, letting the flavour settle on his tongue first before adding. "No, not lemons... but something fruity. What fruit is it, Satariel?"

"It is in the name – blueberry honey," Satariel replied with a smile, licking at his sticky lips and pushing the cork back into the jar. "You can get blackberry honey too, but they do not grow those berries down in the village. Do you like it, little angel?"

"Hmm, I have liked all of the honeys," Miel admitted, running his tongue around his mouth and tasting the mixture of lingering remains. "They have been sweet so far, but that one looks very different to me."

The sample in particular that Miel was talking about was a shocking colour – a shade so dark in the dusky lighting of the glen that it looked black to his eyes. He had never seen honey of such a deep colour before, and he could not help but stare at it as Satariel pulled the cork stopper out.

"Can I look at it, Satariel?" Miel asked, holding his hands out for the jar.

Upon closer inspection, Miel saw there were red tones hidden away inside the dark honey, it was just hard to see them. He had to hold the jar up to the light to see it, and then he sniffed at the honey to find it had a pungent and equally fascinating scent. When he slathered it into his fingers, he was able to see the different tones much more clearly, and so he sucked it free to let it settle on his tongue.

"What type of honey is this, Satariel? It is so unusual,"

Miel remarked, as he was tasting something that he had never tasted before and had no possible words to describe. "It is not that sweet at all!"

"Buckwheat honey," the dæmon replied, scooping his own serving of honey free and shoving his fingers into his mouth.

"What is this new flavour? How do you describe it?"

"Malty, maybe smoky, in parts," Satariel explained around his fingers.

"Malty..." Miel repeated, savouring the aftertaste as his friend secured the jar onto his belt to retrieve the final sample of honey.

"I saved the best one until last. Sourwood, because I know that you will love this one the most," Satariel said with a confident smile, popping the stopper free and holding the jar out to him. "Taste it, little angel."

The final jar of honey was a creamy, golden shade that was lighter than the others. It looked as different to what he had thought honey looked like as the dark buckwheat variety had been. Miel was instantly attracted to the sight of the sourwood honey because he thought it looked milky and sweet, and so he lifted his hand to dip his finger into the mixture and lick it free.

Oh, the taste of this honey was so sweet and buttery that it made Miel's lips curve upwards at the corners.

Satariel was right, this *was* his favourite honey flavour out of all the choices, and he made a series of pleased hums as he let it settle on his tongue before swallowing it.

"It is so tasty, Satariel!" Miel exclaimed. "The name sounds so unpleasant, but it tastes so creamy and sweet!"

"Ah, now we know your favourite honey," Satariel said with a fond smile, as he stuck his fingers into the jar to get his own taste of it. "It is one of my favourites too, and–"

Miel leaned forward to catch his fingers in his mouth before he could sample the delicacy, and he cheekily sucked the sourwood honey free and saw Satariel's eyes growing massive in surprise. But then his friend started laughing because he found his naughty antics highly amusing.

As an apology for stealing the honey from him, Miel got

more of the sweet treat onto his forefinger and held it out to him in offering.

Satariel parted his lips for him, but rather than let him lick or suck it free from his finger, Miel dabbed the honey right onto his nose. The dæmon blinked hard in surprise, a blob of milky honey smeared right there on the end of his rounded nose.

"Ah, such a naughty little angel!" Satariel exclaimed, before shoving his fingers into the jar again.

Within seconds, they were playfully chasing dribbles of honey down each other's wrists and sucking on each other's fingers – giggling the entire time. Miel had smears of honey all over his cheeks and chin, sticky and sweet, and Satariel's bare knees and thighs were also covered in fat droplets of the creamy nectar.

The jar was small, and so there was only a little amount of honey inside it. By the time that their moment of mischief had passed, there was little more than smears of the substance coating the sides of the glass jar, for the rest of the honey had gone straight into their bellies and all over their faces.

Whilst Miel tried to clean his sticky cheeks, Satariel retrieved his pouch of snacks, which he unknotted to start rummaging through the different things that he had gathered. Like last time, it was packed with nuts, berries, flower heads, and beetles.

Miel watched him gathering up a palmful of things before retrieving the jar of light, golden wildflower honey to drizzle it onto them. "Satariel?"

"Mmm, little angel?" Satariel asked, munching the handful of honey-soaked nuts and berries happily before licking at his palm to clean up the sticky treat.

"I brought you something too," Miel admitted, as he reached inside of his tunic and pulled free his surprise gift. "I hope that you like them, I made them just for you."

"What... what are they?" he asked, shifting to place his pouch in his lap and eyeing the two golden, braided threads that were dangling from his hands.

"I thought... well, I thought that your horns would be perfect to display things on," Miel explained in a soft voice. "So, whilst I was singing praise at dawn, I decided to make these for you."

After a moment, Satariel sucked his fingers free of sticky berry juice and honey, and then he wiped them on his tunic to fully clean them. He could now touch one of the decorations without sullying them, and he held it in both of his hands to study the object intently.

One end of the thread had been knotted into a loop so that it could be slipped around his little horns, and the lengths had been decorated with a multitude of his moulted feathers that Miel had carefully sewn into place.

Satariel stroked the different coloured feathers with his fingertips, feeling the smooth and tough ones, and the fluffy and soft ones, and then he glanced up at him.

"Like this," Miel suggested, moving to slowly slip the decoration around his right horn for him and then pulling it down to the base.

Miel sat back to study his dæmon friend, seeing the way that the braided thread dangled down to his shoulder – much like the beautiful hair pins and accessories that mortal women wore.

"Ah, Satariel!"

"What?"

Satariel had just secured the second decoration in place on his left horn, and at this sudden declaration, he froze in place. His eyes grew round with surprise, his fingers tightening around the feathery braid as he waited for him to speak.

"Satariel, you look... adorable!" Miel exclaimed, clapping his hands against his chest just as a burst of giggles escaped him.

"Huh?" Satariel hummed, dropping his hands into his lap and cocking his head at him. The movement caused the decorations to shift, dangling around his rounded face in the sweetest of ways. "Adorable?"

"Such an adorable, little dæmon!" Miel remarked, and he struggled to suppress the urge to reach over and cup his full cheeks in his hands.

This compliment was enough to make Satariel's face

diffuse with a ruddy redness, which he tried his hardest to hide behind his own hands. It was a worthy attempt, but Miel could see the colour through the cracks in his fingers. The way that his cheeks squished up to make his eyes narrow into slits just made him look that little bit more adorable, and Miel could not help but carry on giggling at him.

"Miel, you are as sweet as sourwood honey," Satariel mumbled in a quiet voice, his face mostly hidden behind his hands.

"I... I am?" Miel asked in a soft voice, as he reached over to pluck a carnation head from his friend's pouch and popped it into his mouth to chew.

Satariel just made a noise at this rather than speak, and he slowly lowered his hands from his flushed cheeks to reveal he had a happy smile on his face.

The way that his decorative braids gently danced from the movement was highly pleasing, and Miel thought they framed his rounded face so perfectly – his golden, pink, and white feathers clashing against his blue-tinged hair.

"Little angel, we should go down into the village," Satariel said so suddenly, catching him by total surprise. "It could be fun, do you not think so?"

"Huh? Go into the village? With... with the mortals?" Miel asked in a soft voice, watching him securing the empty glass jar onto his belt again. "But I have never been to the village before, Satariel, I do not know if... if I should."

"Why not?" the dæmon asked curiously, as his fingers pulled the twine tight to leave the jar dangling around his hips.

Yet, Miel did not know what to say in response to this question. He had many thoughts racing through his mind, but not a single one seemed fit to say aloud, and so he just held his tongue and left his friend to break their momentary silence.

"Miel, there are so many things for you to taste in the village," Satariel explained, as he shifted his weight onto his knees and took hold of his hands. "Fruits, vegetables, crops – so many delectable treats for you to sample."

"I know, but the mortals, Satariel," Miel replied, dropping his head to avoid his gaze. "I have never seen them before, not in the village. I only see mortal babes when they come here to play. I do not know if I can go down the mountain to see them."

"Are you frightened, little angel?"

"I suppose that I am, in a way," he admitted. "Do you think that is foolish?"

"I do not think it is foolish at all. Fear is a powerful thing, little angel, and I doubt that you have ever really felt it before – save for the first time that we met one another."

Miel made a noise in agreement at this, for Satariel was right – he *had not* felt much fear before, if he had ever really felt it in the first place. Meeting Satariel had made him more nervous than scared, and what he was feeling right now was very similar to that sensation.

"I was frightened to enter the cave this dawn and tend to the shrine. But I did so because I trust you," Satariel continued, as he gave his hands a tight squeeze. "You told me that being inside would not hurt me, and you were right. I could sweep inside the cave, and touch the very shrine inside. There was nothing for me to fear, save for my own imagination. So, what are you frightened of, little angel?"

"It is not about the mortals or anything like that, Satariel, it is more just... the new experience; I think?" Miel explained with a soft shrug, his wings twitching as he did so. "I was a little bit scared to taste those flowers too. But I did so because you told me just how wonderful taste was – and I just knew that I had to experience it for myself. Is... is there really lots of things to taste in the village?"

At this question, Satariel shifted to get to his feet, and then he held his hand out to him in offering.

Miel took hold of his hand and let him gently tug him upright, guiding him across the clearing again to presumably head off in the direction of the mortal village at the base of the mountain.

"Little angel, there is so many things for you to sample," Satariel explained, glancing back over his shoulder at him as they ducked beneath the branches. "Like I said, the mortals grow crops for fields on end, and they have these large areas where they sell hot goods for other mortals to eat – like meaty broths and spicy soups! During the morning hours, the village smells so wonderful and enticing! But I think that the orchard is where you will want to visit."

Just like at dawn, Satariel escorted him through the woods by way of taking several winding paths through the thick copses of trees. Miel had never been to the village, and so he had no clue where they were going, he just knew that the dæmon would get them both there without getting lost.

The paths were dark and narrow, the ground scratchy and dry beneath their feet, and filled with dry twigs and tiny animal bones. There were not many flowers present at all, though there was thick growths of leafy plants and shrubs.

Eventually, the path in front of them opened up into a wide, sloping hill, at the bottom of which the mountain stream flowed into a wide trench that the mortals had built a wooden bridge across.

So, this was how the mortal babes got to and from the village!

It was so clever, and Miel wondered if the little ledges along the outside of the bridge were so that the mortals could also fish in the deep and clear brook waters, or perhaps comb for seaweed and other little creatures – like mussels and abalone.

Miel could see the village across the stretch of field, the outskirts of which were filled with many rows of small cottages that had smoke coming from their stone chimneys, and glass-filled windows that were glowing a dim orange that signalled the mortals were inside them. There was faint noise coming from the village, which mingled with the even softer sounds of distant livestock still out in the local farmland. He stopped for a moment to study the sight of the village.

"Little angel, are you ready to go see the village?" Satariel asked, as he gave his hand a soft squeeze.

"I... I am ready, my dearest dæmon."

Rather than make their way down the hill to get to the bridge, Miel swept Satariel up into his arms and beat his wings hard enough to propel them both into the air. He did not shoot upwards into the sky, for he stayed low and hooked his arms underneath Satariel's armpits; cradling his chest and burying his cheek against the warm and soft slope of his neck. He flew them down the hill and to the stream, dipping down low so that his friend could skirt the surface of the water with his feet.

Satariel's toes stepped down into the stream and created violent ripples, and fat droplets formed on them that splashed in all directions. It was as if he was running on the surface of the water, and the dæmon giddily laughed from the sensation. Just feeling his thin chest vibrating with each happy guffaw made Miel start giggling too; their laughter echoing on the still evening air.

As soon as Miel placed him down on the other side of the stream, Satariel hunkered down to eye his reflection in the surface of the water. It was still covered in ripples from his dipping toes, but after a moment, it settled down so that he could look at himself.

Upon catching sight of his horn decorations, Satariel made a series of noises that sounded caught between amusement, embarrassment, and happiness to Miel's ears. Then he reached up to touch them, fingering the feathers before brushing them back behind his ears.

"We can walk through the village, if you wish? Or we can stick to the outskirts and enter the farmland instead?" Satariel suggested, as he straightened up again and took hold of his hand. "At night, the village can be very quiet and still. We might not see many mortals at all, but we might see their dogs guarding their homes."

"We can walk through it, at least until we are close to the farmland," Miel replied, letting the dæmon take the lead once more to guide him into the village. "I want to see what it looks like, now that we are here. I do not feel frightened right now, not with you here, Satariel."

"Well then, let us go for a walk, little angel."

Miel was to find that the village was built in a very neat manner: with wide dirt roads between the cottages and small walls of stone and wood to designate each property's borders. It was not cramped or messy, but carefully constructed, and he enjoyed looking at the cream, wood and thatch exteriors of the houses as they passed them by.

Much like Satariel had remarked, they did not see many mortals at all, save for some elderly-looking women that seemed to be washing clothing in large tubs on boards. They had richly tanned skin from years of being out in the sun working the fields, and wizened but motherly-looking faces. Their greying hair was gathered together and hidden beneath fascinating hair scarves.

But they did see several different dogs lying under the porches to guard the houses and stay warm from the heat of the stoves. They were either wolf-like, with pointed ears, muscular bodies and brush tails in shades of white, grey, and black and tan; or they were shaggy things that looked to have thick, soft fur with lolling pink tongues.

It was as they were passing through a large square that Satariel suddenly picked up speed. He pulled him over to a deep wooden crate that looked to be filled with goods.

"This is an apple, little angel," Satariel declared, as he snatched up three of the small fruits from the crate and proceeded to juggle them. "If you enjoyed the tastes of the flowers, you will adore how these taste."

"I will?" Miel asked, tracking each of the apples as they first flew up into the air and then gently curved down to land on his palm with a soft slapping sound. Red, then red, then green – over and over in a cycle.

"Red apples are often thought to be sweeter than green, but mortals do not truly understand flavour. They use their eyes too much, and it affects their tongue," Satariel stated, as he stopped juggling the apples to place one of the red ones down on the pile. Then he held the other red one out to him. "Try it, and see what you think; mmm?"

Miel moved to accept the apple from him. He held it between his fingers so delicately, just because he was frightened of bruising the soft and glossy skin.

The apple was shapely, with a gorgeous round body that tapered down to a narrow bottom. Its skin had skeins of gold threaded through it – so that it was not just a solid, deep red. It looked so enticing that he just could not resist the temptation, and so he lifted it to his lips to take a cautious bite.

Satariel watched him eagerly, and there was a glossy green apple held in front of his lips that had yet to be bitten. There was something like sheer awe glinting in his eyes, and his round cheeks were flushed with excitement much akin to his own.

At first, the apple skin resisted against his teeth, but with added pressure, Miel was able to sink them down into the flesh and take his first proper bite. As he pulled his head away, he saw that the flesh was slightly yellow, and he could follow the gentle curve of his teeth around the edges of the bite mark.

Apples, Miel was to find, were softer than they appeared. The flesh turned to mush between his teeth within several slow chews, flooding its juice out onto his tongue much like how the flowers had when he had gnawed on their petals.

"What do you think, little angel?"

Miel swallowed the bite of apple and chased his tongue around his mouth, finding every little hint of sweetness. All he could do was make noises of appreciation because he could not seem to find a way to explain the flavours or sensations.

Unlike honey, which was entirely liquid and able to be swallowed, Miel needed to chew the apple many times – even more times than the soft and small flower heads.

"Here, try the green one too," Satariel suggested, holding it out for him.

Rather than take it in his hold, Miel just leaned forward to take a bite of the apple. This one was most certainly softer than the red apple, and though it had a very similar flavour, there were some differences.

"I think the green one is... is fresh," Miel said around the bite, struggling to find the words to explain the flavours that he was tasting. "There is a crisp flavour, I think? It is not as sweet as the red, but I like it more!"

"You have such a perfect tongue, little angel," Satariel said with a smile, before sinking his teeth down deep into the green apple to take an almighty crunching bite.

As they carried on walking through the village square, they both shared and savoured the apples. Miel found he enjoyed chewing the skin, even when there was a tartness to it, but he obviously loved the soft flesh more. It was hard to explain why he liked eating the apple so much when it had such a clean and mild flavour, but he supposed that the new sensation of *eating* something might just be why he liked it.

When there was nothing but a thin core left, Miel carefully pulled the seeds free to hold them in his palm. They were so tiny, but with care, they could turn into a massive and powerful tree – just like mother creatures raised their young babies into strong adults.

Satariel noticed he was staring at the seeds, and so he retrieved the empty glass jar and popped the cork stopper free. This meant he could place the seeds inside the jar for safekeeping.

"We might just be able to grow a tree from them, little angel," Satariel remarked, holding the jar up to eye the seeds. "Our own apple tree in the glen, so we can harvest their fruits when they bloom, mmm?"

"I would treasure such a tree," Miel said with a happy smile. "A tree grown from the bonds of friendship – ah, I bet that it will grow so tall, Satariel!"

"Taller than the both of us, for sure," Satariel agreed with a mischievous grin.

After walking through the village for some time longer, his dæmonic friend guided him off in the direction of the farmland that surrounded the village. As they traversed through the farmland, Satariel told him about all of the different kinds of crops that the mortals grew in the village.

There was the edible grains and vegetables, such as many varieties of cabbage, radish, onions, carrots, peppers and potatoes; but there were also ones that he said were for making other things. Cotton and hemp; tobacco and tea – the mortals grew so much! Then there was the livestock too, which Miel discovered consisted of: cows, pigs, chickens and ducks, and even goats and sheep. There were horses too, to work the fields and escort the mortals carts, along with dogs and cats to keep out pests and protect their land.

Satariel escorted him around wet and muddy rice

paddies that ran thick and far between the trickling stream tributaries until they were entering fields filled with tall plants. "These are their crops, little angel, which you must know about; mmm?"

"The mortals harvest these crops as they grow, yes? They grow them in the earth and cultivate them for food, for themselves and their livestock?" Miel replied, to which Satariel made a noise in agreement. "These crops are inedible right now, are they not?"

"Ah, these crops are millet, for feeding cows, and not for your tongue to sample. These other crops – corn and buckwheat. The rest of these fields is a wealth of vegetables, like the potatoes, radishes and cabbages that I told you about. But those fields in the distance, the ones with the trees? Can you see them?"

Miel followed his pointing finger to see that Satariel was gesturing at a stretch of land, which was filled with neat rows of trees and several small buildings that might just be homes.

"Fruit trees, little angel! Ripe for the picking!"

With that, Satariel tugged him through the towering field of millet with a cry of excitement. As they ran through the field, the dry husks of the plants slapped against them and rustled loudly, loud enough to cover their giddy laughter. Upon breaking free of the field, their skin and hair was covered in dry specks of husks, and Miel's wings were probably coated in the mess too.

The outskirts of the orchard looked to be where the mortals grew berries and other varieties of creeper and grower plants. The former spread out across the soil, and the latter had been carefully secured to sticks to keep their willowy stems strong. Some of them had white flowers growing alongside their leaves, beside which fat berries had blossomed.

Satariel squatted down to start plucking some of the berries free for him, gathering a selection of juicy and ripe strawberries and blueberries from the flowery bushes that they could sample.

Miel hunkered down beside him and watched him carefully, seeing how he left the green-tinged, smaller fruits alone to continue growing because they were not yet ripe.

With his first taste of a blueberry, Miel discovered it did taste like the blueberry honey had; but it was a different sensation completely. The honey had been thick and strong, but the blueberry was watery and weak. It popped in his mouth when he pressed the berry against the roof of his mouth.

The strawberry, however, was certainly more enticing to him. Biting down into its vibrant red, seeded skin, he found it was soft but firm, and it had a sugary sweet juice.

As they consumed the handful of berries, their fingers and lips were stained from the watery and sticky juices – Satariel's mouth a purple shade from the combination of both fruits. It was very endearing the way that his pouted lips bore the remains of his mischievous berry snatching, and Miel wondered what colour his lips might just be.

When they were finished sampling the berries, Satariel darted off into the orchard to get to the fruit trees.

There was a faint and powerful aroma coming from the rows of trees, which had fruits and blossoms currently dancing in the delicate breeze. A certain hint of fragrance caught Miel's attention, and he realised what it was as he watched the dæmon scaling up a tree trunk.

"So, this is how you find the best honey?!" Miel exclaimed in wonder, as he craned his head back to look at the towering mandarin orange tree. "Orange blossom honey! The blueberry and buckwheat honey! It is from this very orchard!"

"Exactly, little angel!" Satariel called back, as he straddled a thick and gnarled branch with his thin and smooth thighs and plucked a choice orange free.

When he tossed it down, Miel caught it and brought it up to his nose to breathe in the rich scent. Even through the dimpled and thick skin, the intoxicating tang of the juice made him sigh in pleasure.

Satariel clambered back down the tree with startling grace, dropping from branch to branch until he could swing down and land in the grass with a loud *thump.*

Miel accepted the orange from him, and then Satariel started showing him how to peel the skin free to find the tender flesh beneath. His dæmon friend had his sharp teeth to help him ribbon the flesh, but he thought that his nails would do just as good a job.

The segment of orange was so tart that Miel's face scrunched up from the first squirt of juice, which made Satariel laugh heartily.

Ah, the tang in the scent of the blossoms had been a sign of the flavour too.

But even then, Miel liked it a lot. This fruit might be more enjoyable as a juice, squeezed to pulpy liquid rather than trapped within its thin skin.

"Hmm, oranges are wonderful!" Miel declared, shoving another tangy segment into his mouth. "They have so much *flavour,* Satariel! Not like the mild apples at all!"

"You like powerful fruit flavours?" Satariel remarked, as he ran his eyes along the rows of trees to find the next thing to sample. "Many of these fruits can be rather mild, but... what about this one?"

Satariel had to stand on tiptoe to pluck the small but fat fruit from the low branch. It was similar to an apple, save for the fact it was so rounded. Its skin was a wonderful shade of rich orange with red undertones to it, which was smooth and glossy, and it felt soft rather than firm.

As Miel watched him, Satariel lifted the fruit to his mouth, and he tore free the little green stem to open up the fruit. Then he started ribboning at the skin with his sharp teeth, peeling a wide and thick strip down to reveal to him the watery flesh inside.

"What is that, Satariel?"

"A persimmon," he explained, as he sucked up the ribbon of skin and started gnawing on it. "Try it, little angel."

Miel leaned forward to sink his teeth into the fruit, having to suck up quite a chunk of it because it was so watery. The first thing that hit him was a sudden sweetness, so unexpected because of the light scent that it gave off. The persimmon might look to be mild, but it was the sweetest fruit that he had sampled so far.

"Oh, so sweet!" Miel cried out, wiping at his slick chin to

chase after the sticky and sweet nectar of the persimmon and suck it all up from his fingers. "I thought it would be gentle, but that is such a sweet juice!"

Satariel chewed up the skin of the persimmon before taking his own sucking bite of the flesh, making pleased sounds as he did so.

Oh, the explosions of tastes on his tongue were unlike anything that Miel had ever imagined.

With every bite of a succulent berry or crisp crunch of tight fruit skin, he was overwhelmed by the duality of the flavour and the liquid settling onto his tongue. He wanted to taste everything that Satariel plucked free, from the oranges and persimmons, to the fat and creamy pears, and the mild and crisp apples.

There was not a single fruit that he did not want to sample, just like the honey, and all his momentary nerves about coming down into the village had been simply washed away.

Skipping through the orchard with Satariel, feeding each other bites of juicy fruit and climbing up to swing from the branches and hugging the broad and rough trunks of the trees, Miel felt nothing close to fear – just sheer elation.

"Peaches! Satariel, they have peaches!" Miel cried out in excitement, eyeing the white and pink skins dangling from the branches above them.

Even when he had never tasted them before, Miel knew that peaches just *had* to be tasty because they smelled so beautiful. He had smelled wild peaches up in the woods, and he loved inhaling their scent and watching the little creatures sniffing and nibbling at them.

"The ripest fruit are at the top of the branches, little angel!" Satariel remarked, before letting out a giddy chuckle and covering his grinning mouth.

Miel did not need to hear that again, for he gave his wings a hard beat to take to the air and soar right up to the top of the peach tree. As he reached the top, he snatched one of the fruits, and he felt a soft ripeness in his fist as he circled around the branches and dived back down to join his laughing friend.

Satariel was laughing so much that he was almost gasping for breath, and Miel had just dropped to land beside him when he saw something completely unexpected.

There was a mortal standing right there in the field, staring at the two of them with a slack expression.

Miel froze in surprise at the sight of the mortal, his smile faltering at the corners.

It took him a moment to realise that the mortal was not looking *at* them exactly, rather looking past them because she could not truly see them.

She could probably sense something coming from their direction – maybe noticing the rippling grass, or sensing a wave of light or heat coming from them both, but she certainly could not see them.

"Satariel," Miel whispered out the corner of his mouth. "Look."

Satariel turned to look back over his shoulder, and he also caught sight of the mortal that almost seemed to be looking at them.

Miel could see she was a girl, a tall girl that might just be considered a woman. It was hard ascertaining her age in the dim glow from the lantern that she was carrying, but he could see she had large and round eyes, and her hair was currently hanging loose down past her shoulders. She was clad in a loose white cotton dress, with a thick blue blanket tossed over her shoulders.

Perhaps, she had been preparing for sleep before something had caught her attention and had made her leave the cottage across the orchard?

Satariel snatched another fat peach from the spindly branch right above their heads, and then he darted across the field. Miel was tugged along behind him because he was holding onto his wrist, and he could not help but burst into giggles as his friend dragged them both into a bush to hide from the mortal. They settled down behind it, peeping at her through the gaps in the foliage as mischievous as mortal babes.

"Huh? Where did it go?" the girl mumbled, as she slowly

shifted her gaze across the field and seemingly tracked them.

"Nell?! Where have you wandered off to now?!"

A male voice cut through the air as sharp as a blade, catching them all by surprise. Even in the evening dusk, Miel could see the girl's large eyes wincing at the corners, and her blanket-clad shoulders lifted in a skittish jump at the sudden sound.

"I... I thought that I saw something out in the field, brother!" she called. She did not turn to look back over her shoulder, but rather just stared out across the field where they had been frolicking.

"Something like what exactly, Nell?" the boy asked, coming to a stop beside her and placing his hands on his hips.

In the light from the lantern, Miel could see that this boy was a little shorter than she was, and his hair was gathered up in parts in a knot to reveal his rather handsome face. He was also wearing something that looked like a dress for sleeping in, though he had thrown a jacket over it to keep away the chill.

"I do not know, Blake, it sounds rather silly if I say it aloud, but... I saw a light out there, a bright light, and it was dancing around and–"

"Ah, are you playing a game with me? You saw a firefly, Nell!" Blake declared, giving Nell a wide and mischievous grin that revealed many white teeth.

The grin showed to Miel that these mortals were as close as kin could be. There was something so delightfully wonderful in the way that they spoke and looked at each other – a deep bond for sure.

"No, not a firefly! It was so much bigger and brighter!" Nell argued, lifting her hand that was holding the lantern and shaking it for emphasis. *"It might have been the size of this, if not bigger! That is not a firefly, brother, it was far too big for that!"*

Miel could feel his friend shaking beside him, and when he turned his head to look at him, he saw that Satariel was trying to not laugh at the mortals. He was trying so very hard too, his shoulders rising and falling as breathy wheezes escaped him; his lips pulled back in a wide grin that showed every single one of his sharp teeth, and his eyes deeply crinkled at the corners.

Just looking at him made Miel start laughing too, and he lifted his hand to cover his own lips in a bid at suppressing his giggles. There was no need to do so because the mortals could not hear or even see them, but there was just something so mischievous about laughing at their confusion and bickering.

"It flew all around the peach tree. But before then, it was moving all around the trees; almost like it was dancing," Nell finished, lowering her hand again and letting out a series of frustrated noises.

"You know what, Nell? You might just have seen a fairy, a beautiful fairy come down from the fairy world. She might just have fallen in love with you and—"

Nell reached over to give Blake a hard shove at this, their clothing rustling loudly from the movement. Miel heard the *thump* of her hand slamming against the boy's chest, and judging from the way that he stumbled backwards from the push, it was far from gentle.

But the shove just made Blake laugh, clearly finding her reaction amusing. Ah, for mortals that looked almost to be full adults grown, they were so childish when no one was present to keep them in check.

"Or, maybe it was an angel, hmm? They come down from heaven on rainbows. Is there a rainbow out this evening?"

Blake threw a hand up to press it against his brow at this, leaning back and squinting up at the dusky evening sky as if searching for this elusive rainbow. Ah, he was a naughty mortal indeed, and he was going to earn himself another hard shove from Nell if he did not stop his antics.

"Ah, you are hopeless, Blake," Nell muttered, as she reached over to link her arm through the boy's and she held onto him. *"Come on, we should head back inside. It must just have been my imagination or something, you know how strong it can get."*

The pilfered peach tasted just as sweet as Miel had been hoping it would have. As he bit into it, he watched the two mortals walking away and listened to their soft voices. The peach was most certainly worth flying up to the top branches to retrieve, and he thought it might just be his favourite fruit that he had sampled this evening.

Satariel was sitting there beside him, his legs cocked up in front of him with the other peach held between his greedy and sticky little fingers. He looked so delightfully naughty and pleased with himself that Miel could feel an overwhelming wave of fondness for the mischievous dæmon.

There were no words that could truly explain the sensation that Satariel stirred deep within his breast, for not even Miel's eons of knowledge could seem to understand the feeling. It was close to the satisfaction that praise gave him, but it did not seem right that the dæmon could make him feel such a thing.

All Miel knew was that looking at Satariel filled him with a warmth that made him feel so happy, so content and at peace. Before he could help himself, he moved to press his mouth against his cheek.

When Miel's lips brushed against his skin, he felt a warmth trapped within the rounded apple of his cheek that was so unexpected, but also so perfect. The kiss made Satariel's shoulders tense up in surprise, and he turned his head to look at him with those black and rounded eyes of his before lowering his focus onto his lips.

After a moment of hesitation, Satariel leaned forward so slowly that Miel could feel himself almost shaking in anticipation until he felt the dæmon's lips against his.

At first, it was nothing more than a soft brush of skin against skin, but then Satariel pouted his lips out so he could apply pressure against his mouth.

Miel copied his actions, feeling his lips slipping to catch his lower lip between them both. It was tender and wet from fruit juice, but also chapped from his sharp, nibbling teeth.

When his friend pulled his face away, a soft sound came from their lips, but that was not enough for Miel. He wanted to feel something *more* than just his skin, and so he brought their lips together again… and again, and again – until Satariel was making breathy noises and his lips parted enough for Miel to open his mouth with every kiss.

They had explored tastes with their mouths, just like they had explored touch with their fingers, and scent with their noses. Just like how they had skittered their fingertips across the soles of their feet and had tickled at their toes; like how they had traced their thumbs over the bumps of their knuckles, and had tangled their fingers together – they were simply investigating more sensations with their mouths.

But the kisses felt different to Miel in a way he quite simply could not understand. This was not like the flowers and honey settling on his tongue, the damp soil and blood flooding his nose, this was different – and he knew that Satariel could feel it too. This... powerful warmth and elation coursing through his body that had no word to possibly describe it.

Just like how he had been able to smell the blood and soil on his fingers, Miel could smell *and* taste the fruit on Satariel's tongue. It was not as powerful as the juices had been when he had bitten into the fruits, for it was rather a faded ghost of the taste. But he still licked at his tongue as hungrily as he had licked honey free from his friend's fingers; feeling Satariel's broad tongue curling to a point to flick at his lower lip.

The peaches dropped from their grips so they could take hold of each other: Miel's one landing in the soil with a soft *thump*, and Satariel's one bursting open on his thighs with a juicy *splat* that made the sweet scent waft up to their noses.

Miel instinctively took hold of his cheek in one hand, his other hand settling on his neck, and Satariel's fumbling fingers found his upper arms to hold onto him tightly.

Satariel finally broke the contact by pulling his face away first, his eyes closed as he tried to catch his breath.

Miel moved to press his lips against his cheek instead, just so he could carry on kissing him. The dæmon's lips were flushed and slick, and his cheeks were filled with colour and heat that he could almost feel radiating from his skin.

"Little angel, you... you *do* taste sweeter than sourwood honey," Satariel sighed out, and his arms slipped around his neck to pull him close and hold onto him. His hand found his wing, and he stroked it across the bone tenderly in a way that made him ruffle the feathers hard. "I should have... should have known that angel lips would taste that sweet."

"Dæmon lips taste better than flowers, honeys, *and* fruits," Miel declared enthusiastically, and he brought his lips away from his cheeks just in time to see his pleased smile. "I just want to keep tasting them, Satariel; why can I not seem to stop?!"

Satariel could only laugh at this, his body weakly shaking in his hold and his sweet breath hitting against his face.

Why did Miel want to kiss him so much, he did not at all know. Angels were incapable of feeling such urges like love and romance because of their inability to copulate, and yet he could not seem to fight the longing to bring his lips to Satariel's and kiss him over and over.

The contact just filled him with a happiness unlike any other – a happiness that he was starting to think might just be love for his dæmonic friend.

When Miel started kissing him again, Satariel almost melted into his hold – eager to return the deep and exploratory kisses. His fingers teased at his wings playfully, ruffling the feathers until Miel found one of his horns and gave it a soft knead.

Oh, Satariel shuddered at this, and he moaned into his mouth with a longing that showed the true depth of his emotions.

Miel lost track of how many kisses they shared in the orchard bushes; covered in sticky fruit juices and rich soil. But it was the bracing scent of wind that made him finally relent and stop kissing him.

"I can smell rain, my dearest dæmon," Miel explained, as his thumb found his lips and stroked across them. "We should head back to the woods, find shelter from it – just in case."

On the walk through the village and back into the mountain woods, they collected together a random assortment of fruits and wildflowers so they could enjoy them. Satariel carried them in the skirt of his tunic, holding the ends up to flash most of his thighs.

Miel still loved sampling bites of orange, persimmon, and

peach, but he found that their flavours did not create the same burst of excitement as they had done so earlier.

Not after he had tasted Satariel's lips.

They were deep within the woods when the sudden *crack* of thunder reverberated through the air and made Miel jump in shock. The remains of his orange dropped to land in the soil, a grand treat for the bugs in the dirt that would love its sugary juices.

The sound of rainfall followed it seconds later, the thick foliage catching most of the rain so that it did not drop down to hit them. They had to stick close to the tree trunks to save themselves from the occasional drizzle. The temperature was still warm within the woods, but it would lower by several degrees over the course of the storm.

Upon stepping into the glen, the rain was pelting down at the tremendous strength, bouncing off the soil with thundering sound that rivalled the *boom* and *crack* of the actual thunder itself.

Just like Miel had imagined, Satariel did indeed use the pussy willow for shelter from the elements. There was a massive hollow in the back that could easily fit multiple animals, and they could build a den within its trunk.

Satariel burrowed deep inside the willow trunk, and he pulled him inside with him so they could shelter from the downpour of rain before they were soaked through to the skin.

Within seconds, the cool air of the den warmed up from their bodies, turning the shelter into a cosy hole, rather than a dank and cold one.

Miel spread his wings and then curled them around their bodies, helping to trap the heat and stop any gusts of air from blowing inside of their little sanctuary. He knew that within the protective barrier of his wings, and the strong and warm press of his friend's arms, he was safe from the storm.

Satariel's soft lips found his own even in the darkness of the trunk, just so he could give him tender and deep kisses until his fear melted away just like honey on his tongue.

V.

The weight of the reed bucket was starting to make his arms ache. The contents sloshed around to hit against the sides and luckily did not spill free all over his filthy, bare feet.

Satariel had been carrying it through the woods for quite some time now, having collected the water straight from the waterfalls up the mountain path to ensure he had clean and pure water. He was so close to the glen that he did not need to carry it much longer.

Whilst Miel had been slumbering within the pussy willow trunk, Satariel had went on an extensive walk through the woods to retrieve several things for the day.

First, Satariel had scavenged for meat of some kind to fill his hollow belly with – having found a dead deer from which to gorge on her still steaming and bloody entrails. Then he had retrieved a bouquet of wild roses from the flower patch to leave for Miel when he woke up. Finally, he had collected the bucket of water, and he was in the act of carrying it back into the glen for them to use.

Satariel did not really know how or why, but even after he had spent a long time away from Miel's radiance and wings in the cool woods, he still felt *warm* deep down inside his chest.

It was as if the angel had set his very core alight with his affections and friendship, and he would have skipped back to the glen had it been possible. But the bucket was just too heavy for that, and he did not want to upend the contents all over the ground.

Miel emerged from the willow trunk just as he entered the glen again, slowly crawling out and squinting at the dawn sunlight through his soft eyelashes. The sight of the angel brought a pleased smile to Satariel's face as he lugged the bucket right over to the tree.

"I brought us some mountain water," Satariel explained, as he lowered the bucket to the ground and sat down in the grass. "To clean our faces, hands, and feet. We are very dirty, little angel."

"Hmm?" Miel hummed, rolling his head back to stretch his stiff muscles and then spreading his wings out to their fullest extent. He reached up to rub at his swollen eyelids with his still sticky fists, which Satariel knew to smell sweet, like peaches and strawberries. "Satariel?"

"Yes, little angel?" he asked, as he shifted to lean closer to him.

Miel turned his head to bring their lips together in a kiss, catching Satariel by surprise and making his breath catch in his throat. But then he relaxed and pouted his mouth out in return, opening his lips so that the angel's tongue could find his own and make shivers of exaltation run down his spine.

"You taste like... like green apples," Miel remarked in a soft voice, before letting out a breathless laugh. "Did you eat some apples, Satariel?"

"You can... can taste apples?" Satariel asked in shock, pulling his head back in an attempt at holding his eyes. It was hard doing so when the angel was holding onto the back of his neck. "How did you taste them, little angel?"

"I could taste them on your tongue," he whispered in reply, his lips lifting in a wicked smile that made his eyes crinkle deeply at the corners.

"I did not eat any green apples, but I did eat some roses," Satariel explained, softly bumping their noses together. "I can smell them on you too, little angel, and you taste like–like–"

Satariel stopped talking so he could bring their mouths together again; Miel's lips already parted wide in anticipation of his exploring tongue.

"Strawberry and mint!" Satariel declared confidently after breaking the kiss. "I am not the only one that ate the roses! You must have eaten some too!"

"Well, there was a little bouquet of them right beside my face when I awoke from my slumber, my dearest dæmon, so... I decided to eat them," Miel explained with a sheepish expression, his wings ruffling as he reached up to start playing with one of his horn decorations.

"They were a gift, not breakfast! But if you wanted to eat them, little angel, I hope that you enjoyed them."

Satariel let Miel play with the golden braid and feathers, whilst he just stayed close and absorbed his warmth and breathed in his scent.

Hibiscus, peach, and roses – such a beautiful combination from a beautiful being. The angel might just be covered in soil and sticky patches of fruit juice, but he looked so radiant in the early dawn sunlight that Satariel could not help but feel waves of fondness swelling in his chest.

Miel was his *friend* – even when he was a lowly dæmon.

Miel thought he was adorable, and that his lips tasted sweeter than nectar and honey, and Satariel was so in love with the angelic being that his very soul was aflame with passion.

Miel took a deep inhale, and he held it in his lungs for a moment before letting it out again in a sigh. The scent of petrichor hung heavy in the air, a fresh and heady perfume that would forever remind Satariel of meeting him that one fateful dusk.

"Ah, the soil is rich with moisture today! The flowers and fruit trees must be very happy!" Miel declared with a bright smile, his full and pink cheeks glowing in a dewy fashion. "Satariel, do you still have those seeds? We *must* try and plant them now that the earth is so fertile for them."

"Of course, I do, little angel," he confirmed, turning his head to glance across the glen to find a nice spot to plant them.

Satariel moved to hunker down in a good spot, and he dug a little furrow into the damp soil before retrieving his jar from his belt and pulling the cork stopper free. He tipped the seeds into his palm, and then he gently placed them into the furrow, ready to plant them into the rain-soaked and rich black soil.

Miel moved to hunker down behind him and slipped his arms around his waist, taking hold of his hands so they could finish planting the seeds together.

The angel's body was so warm against his, his chin digging into his shoulder, and his hands settling on top of his.

"With time, it will become the tallest and most beautiful apple tree of them all, my precious, little angel," Satariel sighed, as they patted the soil in place and then entwined their fingers together tight. "We will tend to it every single dawn, give it love and water so that it can grow strong."

"Just like our friendship?" Miel remarked, as he turned his head and pressed a soft kiss against the apple of his cheek.

"Mmm, like our love, little angel," he agreed, nuzzling his nose against his lips with a smile.

"Can we collect more seeds, beautiful dæmon? I want to grow our very own orchard right here in the glen," Miel suggested, and he lifted one of his hands to sweep it through the air and gesture at all the room that they had to work with. "Fruit trees, berries and vegetables – we can harvest them here, and the mortal babes can savour them too. Maybe we will get our own bee hives close-by, to make honey from; hmm? It can be our own sanctuary, just for the two of us."

"That would be perfect, Miel..."